The WICKETT SISTERS

In Jahannam

The WICKETT SISTERS

In Jahannam

STEPHEN HOUSER

I need noise
I need the buzz of saw
Need the crack of a whip
Need some blood in the cut

— K. Flay —
Blood in the Cut

All I'm askin' is for a little respect,
R-E-S-P-E-C-T, R-E-S-P-E-C-T!

— Aretha Franklin —
Respect

CHAPTER ONE

Mardie sat at the table surveying her kitchen. There were maple cupboards stained dark and rich. A butcher-block island. Dutch blue-and-white tile counter backsplashes with scenes of children skating on frozen canals. Cheerful lace curtains with embroidered daisies and tulips hanging on her one narrow window. An antique wooden ice box that was altogether more reliable than any refrigerator she'd ever owned. And best of all, her beloved stove, a cast iron *Andre Godin* from France. It was done in black enamel with copper knobs, a brass-plated door, and gold-and-silver curlicues painted in its nooks and crannies.

Mardie picked up the tea kettle, filled it at the sink, and set it on a burner. She opened the stove door and poked the embers. A small array of flames sprang up. When the water boiled, she filled her teacup with hot water, tossed in a big pinch of Twinings tea, and set the cup and saucer on the table, its marquetry surface of Spanish woods protected by a slab of glass.

She had invited her twin sister Mili over to eat cake balls dipped in melted chocolate. She had never cared for Swiss bankers like Lombard Odier. Nor Swiss reformers like Ulrich Zwingli. But she did have a thing for the Swiss restauranteurs like the one who invented chocolate fondue, Conrad Egli. *And* for Americans Robin Ankeny and Charlotte Lyon whose Cake Ball Company's perfect vanilla cake balls were delivered directly to her doorstep every week. By demons. Compliments of her brother-in-law, her sister's husband Lucifer, who'd been restored by Jehovah to the rank of Archangel and charged with doing good throughout God's Creation. Doing good *and* ruling Hell. Not as different from each other as it might seem.

Hell was being renovated by Lucifer in partnership with the righteous work of the residents of the Ben-Yehuda Kibbutz. Millions of acres of irrigated land grew wheat, barley, beans, and tobacco. Orchards of citrus and nuts were everywhere, and hundreds of thousands of truck farm acres filled Hell's supermarkets with fresh vegetables.

The sun shined every day and the industrious kibbutzniks had also planted vast forests and dug enough artificial lakes to surpass Minnesota's fabled ten thousand. Hell's cities and towns had been restored. Abundant jobs existed for those who wanted to work. And every freeway, road, alley, and sidewalk had been repaired and restored.

Want a hamburger? In-N-Out stores were everywhere. How about ice cream? Ben and Jerry's shops were within walking distance no matter where you lived. Born and raised in Hell and want your own baby? Doctors will help you bring a child into the underworld. Not ready for a baby? Candy's Condom outlets will help you *not* bring a child into Hell.

Hell was a place of enormous freedom, with booze and sex for the unrepentant, and churches and clubs with Bible story re-enactments for the pious. All in all, most people had infinitely better lives in Hell than they'd ever had on Earth. Plus, it was a peaceful and safe place. Almost always. Violence occasionally upset the happy status quo. But it had been almost ten years since there had been an incident, and five years since Mardie and her sister Mili had a case to solve, and *that* one had been up in Heaven.

So, it was cake balls to celebrate life. She had four boxes with twelve balls in each one and enough Toblerone chocolate to make sure that every ball was triple-dipped for goodness. And deliciousness. And all of this in Hell. Who could possibly have known? Mardie smiled and waited for her sister Mili, sipping her tea like a proper British lady. Which she was not. Didn't matter. She knew that not a single one of those uppity dames would dare allow themselves to eat twenty-four cake balls. But she would. Viva la difference.

✳ ✳ ✳

Dyn Suchland sat on his old brown leather sofa and drinking Brick and Steel beer brewed at a small distillery in Spokane. He'd found it at a Hells Bells supermarket, and since he'd grown up near Spokane in a little wheat country town named Odessa, he indulged in a little nostalgia and brought a six-pack home.

The label said it had pineapple and grapefruit flavors as well as tropical and citrus undertones. Fuck that shit, he thought and took his first swallow. It had a nice wallop of alcohol and that's all he cared about. That and weightlifting. For a small ugly man, brewskis and weights had been his salvation.

He'd started lifting weights in high school and had continued working out with them during his entire thirty-year career as a Navy SEAL. He still used weights every day down here in Hell. He was short, barely five foot six, and would have been rejected by the SEALs except for the exceptional strength and endurance he had exhibited in the selection process. His first name wasn't really Dyn, but he'd told kids way back in grammar school that it was. He said that it was short for Dynamite. And he'd just kept it.

He had performed over three hundred missions for the US Navy, shooting, choking, chopping, slicing, strangling, and hanging his

3

targets. If his commander would have told him to blow himself up in order to take out the mark, he would have tried his damnedest to do it. Dyn Suchland.

He'd been honorably discharged with eighteen citations for bravery and had lived quite happily—drinking and screwing—until he had fallen out of his pick-up truck drunk and smashed his head open. It was no surprise that he'd wound up in Hell. The surprise was that it was such a great place. He'd gotten a part-time job as a bouncer in a bar, and promptly resumed his life's ambitions—drinking and screwing—with gusto.

Dyn Suchland drank his beer and watched the TV. He was rewatching the sequel to the first John Wick movie. Guns, guts, blood. Perfect matinee fare. Suddenly the door to his studio apartment burst open and two men rushed in. They trained their Russian automatic rifles on him. He knew those weapons. Kovrovskyi AEK-971s. They were long enough to function as accurate distance guns, but also short and light enough to be handled like a pistol. He had used one in Chechnya deployed alongside Russian Spetsnaz special forces. He had killed fifty-three rebels on that mission. His record. The military bean counters had refused to count the six women and three children he'd killed. Pricks. But even without those it was still his personal best as a SEAL.

Suchland stood up slowly, facing the two intruders.

"What do you want?" he asked in a surly tone.

The men stared at him with their weapons leveled, fingers on the triggers. They were dressed in black jeans and black T-shirts. They were lean and they looked Semitic. Black hair and thin, expressionless faces.

"Are you Petty Officer Dyn Suchland?" one of them asked. He pronounced his name as such-land, not *sook*-land as Americans pronounced it. They obviously weren't Americans. And despite carrying their elite pistols, they weren't Russians either.

"Who wants to know?" Dyn responded.

"Sit down," the man ordered. "And we will tell you exactly who wants to know."

* * *

Mili arrived at Mardie's house at the lunch hour. She was dressed in white shorts, a pink halter top, and white Swedish clogs. Mardie greeted her wearing an identical outfit only with white sandals. The twins stared at each other for a moment.

"Your clogs make you look taller than me," Mardie said and hugged her sister.

"Yes," Mili responded, "and they show off my legs, which are, in fact, taller than yours."

Mardie snorted.

"You're pathetic," she said. "Grow up."

"I have," Mili said and chuckled. "By three more inches."

Mardie ignored that and led Mili to the kitchen. The table was set and the fondue pot was filled with chocolate ready to be melted. There was a large, red plastic bowl filled with cake balls. Mili sat.

"Coffee or tea?" Mardie asked her.

"Coffee?" Mili echoed in a disapproving tone. "Do I look like a Yank? Tea, of course."

Mardie poured tea into a cup and placed it on a saucer in front of her sister. She also brought a sugar pot filled to the brim and a small pitcher of heavy cream. She watched Mili stir in lots of both. She sat down to her own tea. Steeped to the point that it was almost black.

"The food is afoot!" Mili declared and served herself a plate full of cake balls. Mardie lit a small can of gel chafing fuel that would burn for two full hours. Mili put a skewer with three cake balls into the melting chocolate. Mardie watched her. Mili smiled contentedly.

Did psychiatrists still declare that each person had an inner child to deal with, Mili wondered? If so, sweets were effective in dealing with her little Mili. She thought that Mardie's inner child wanted smokes, booze, and boys. She suspected that Mardie's inner child was actually an inner teenager. She put a skewer with three cake balls into the chocolate fondue and looked at Mardie.

"Do you miss the hunt, Sis?" she asked.

Mardie looked at Mili.

"Are you referring to the complete dearth of homicide cases for half a decade?" she questioned.

"Yes," Mili answered. "It's terrible to admit I suppose, but I miss the excitement. Seeing Wyatt Earp ride down a slave trader. Hearing Agatha Christie unwind a mystery's shroud. Holding my Derringer trained on Jack the Ripper."

Mardie's face looked both nostalgic and sad.

"I miss those moments," she said quietly.

Mili nodded.

"I also miss poking the cadavers, looking in their wounds, and following the trails of blood." Mili's words made Mardie's face blanch. "The thrill of the chase is nothing if not built on blood, gore, and horror."

Mardie stared silently at her sister. They lifted their skewers out of the chocolate to cool for a moment. They put the cake balls back into the chocolate, but not before Mili snuck a bite from one of her cake balls and licked her lips. Mardie watched her, and then asked her a question.

"So, was an important part of the experience pursuing Jack the Ripper the violence he dealt his female victims? The women who had their throats slit, their vaginas and wombs cut out, and their faces pulled away?" It was a heartless question, but it went to the heart of Mili's fascination with homicidal guts and gore.

"The short answer is yes," Mili responded. "The horror of the murder and mayhem accentuates the urgency of finding the killer and solving the crime."

"And the long answer?" Mardie asked.

"It has to do with keeping the order of things stable and safe. A grisly murder—the kind that makes *you* throw up—sets in high relief the fact that civilization has been torn asunder. That we are suddenly *not* safe to live our lives in their flow and ebb of ordinariness. Some monster has ripped apart our tranquility, threatening us, our children, and our neighbors. Until such a fiend is apprehended, life is chaotic and dangerous. I want to be the one who faces that chaos and rein in the criminal. I want to be the one who restores peace and security. I don't worry about the law. I worry about the order."

✳ ✳ ✳

The crime scene was so bizarre and so bloody that the apartment neighbors who'd entered Dyn Suchland's apartment after hearing a thunderstorm of gunshots called Lucifer's office and asked for his personal involvement. He came. It appeared that every drop of the victim's blood had been emptied from his body. It covered the sofa and the TV, sprayed the walls and floors, and soaked everything around the dead man's cadaver, which lay pale and broken like a shattered China doll.

Lucifer surveyed the horrendous scene and told the Samn demons who'd accompanied him to guard the crime scene until he returned with his wife. He could only see a cyclone path of death. Mili would see the movements of the kill—its beginning, climax, and ending. The Devil shook his head and stepped out of the besieged flat. He would eventually procure a replacement Hellion body for the deceased, but not before Mili determined why anyone wanted this as yet unidentified man dead. And shot completely full of bullets.

✳ ✳ ✳

"More?" Mardie asked, lifting up the empty bowl once full of cake balls.

Mili shook her head.

"I'm too full to even consider the unwise consumption of even one more." She looked at Mardie. "Maybe a cup of coffee after all, though. I'm feeling peckish."

"Peckish?" Mardie asked. "And coffee is the cure?"

"Bill Clinton swears by it."

"My, turning Yankee after all?" Mardie teased.

"Well, yes, in my moment of peckishness anyway," Mili confessed.

Mardie filled her coffee maker with water and added a filter and coffee grounds to the brewing basket. She waited for it to brew as Mili sat idle. Perhaps it was a wicked thing to hope for, but she silently ached for an adventure to fall upon them and cure their ennui. A violent and puzzling adventure. A destructive unraveling of communal life that required Mili and her to save the day.

Mili's mobile rang. She answered it. Mardie cleaned off the table while Mili talked to Lucifer.

"You look troubled, love," Mili told her husband, studying his face on her iPhone monitor.

"Troubled, and shocked," Satan replied. "Whoever said that there was nothing new under the sun clearly never lived in Hell."

"Something terrible has happened?" Mili asked in a hushed voice.

"A man has been murdered. A man who performed dangerous secret missions for the American Navy. Someone came hunting him. His name was Dyn Suchland and he was shot at least a hundred times."

Mili gasped. She'd never heard of such a thing and apparently neither had the Devil.

Mardie felt herself shiver as she filled Mili's coffee cup.

Mili responded to Lucifer.

"You visited the scene?"

"Suchland's neighbors heard the gunfire and discovered his mutilated body. One of them called my office and begged that I see what had happened for myself. I went. I'm back at the office now having folks dig up whatever files we have on the dead man."

"He was damned for his work in the military?"

"Yes. He was a special forces sailor, a SEAL in the US Navy. He killed several dozen people. All of them were perceived as adversaries of the United States government. The dead included women and children."

"Innocents?"

"Collateral damage is what government officials termed it."

"And now someone tracked him down."

"Probably several someones, wielding Russian automatic weapons."

Mili shook her head.

"Did Scotland Yard have a classification for this kind of execution?" Satan asked.

"Yes," Mili answered. "What goes around comes around."

The Devil sighed. That summed up the whole ferocious mess that now faced Mili and Mardie.

"Is the crime scene secure?" Mili asked.

"Yes. Two Samns are keeping it locked down."

My favorite demons, Mardie thought, serving Mili her coffee. She refilled the creamer and topped off the sugar bin.

"Where is the location?" Mili asked.

"Why don't you come to the office and have a look at the photographs the Samns have sent in from the scene? You can also read the files that we pull up on the victim. *Then* we can go to his apartment together." Satan paused, then spoke louder as if to ensure that Mardie could hear him. "Invite Mardie, but warn her that this is the worst carnage that I have ever seen."

Mili looked at Mardie.

She'd heard. She nodded.

Mardie figured she could go to the shot-up apartment if she looked at the crime scene photographs first and got all of her vomiting out of the way. She took a cup out of the cupboard and filled it with coffee. Odd to feel peckish when she'd just gotten the very thing she'd been wishing for.

CHAPTER TWO

Mili and Mardie sat across from Lucifer examining the photographs spread across his desk. They were pictures of Chief Petty Officer Dyn Suchland's body. Mili knew that it was a human corpse only because of the blood and flesh splattered everywhere. His face had been shot away and his body blasted with so many bullets that even the skeleton had been ripped apart. The remains were nothing more than the lumpy outline of a human being.

Mardie had gone to the restroom to throw up twice. She had regretfully brought up the undigested remains of the cake and chocolate she'd eaten before the Devil had called. Her first glance at the photo of the destroyed body of the Navy SEAL had sent her running. She returned to see a close-up of the victim's battered skull. There was no clue that the man had ever had a face. What was left was a skull cavity filled with bone chips and hash. When she came back from the bathroom the second time, she pulled her chair back from Satan's desk and let Mili and Lucifer examine the rest of the photographs on their own.

Who could have done such a thing, Mili wondered? Heartless bastards who could not even relate to their target as a fellow human being? Mercenaries who had murdered men, women, and children their entire

"

lives? Mafia hitmen who never judged a book by its cover other than to make a positive identification and then fill it with bullets? Maybe even relatives of someone the SEAL had assassinated. Desperate brothers or sons avenging themselves on the killer who had ruined their lives.

She and Mardie would find whoever it was. Mili was sure of that. But besides identifying whoever had committed the murder, they had to find out where the assassins were from. She had learned from the Wickett sisters' very first case that the killers could be from anywhere. Hell. Earth. An alternate world. Even Heaven. Where would *these* bastards be from?

Mili leaned back. Lucifer stacked the photos and pushed them to the side of his desk.

"Any eyewitnesses?" Mili asked.

"No," he replied. "Plenty of folks heard the shots, but they arrived after the fact."

"I never saw a person truly shot to pieces before," Mili said.

The Devil nodded. A tanned young man walked into the room wearing khaki shorts and a white short-sleeve dress shirt. He was tall and muscular with dark slicked-back hair, black horn-rim glasses, and lots of tattoos on his arms, neck, and face that looked like aboriginal creatures.

I miss Trump, Mardie thought, watching Lucifer's new assistant. Or Coogan. Or whatever his name turned out to be after she and Mili had changed things by traveling back in time looking for Jack the Ripper. But Trump had been a betrayer, and this was his replacement. He looked like an Ivy League drug dealer. Satan introduced him.

"Ladies, this is Michael Rockefeller." The young man nodded graciously. "He is a brilliant chap who gets everything right the first time. You may not have seen him before as he spent a good deal of his time among the last primitive tribes in New Guinea. Hence the deep tan and the panoply of antediluvian tattoos."

Mardie was impressed with the hunk. Big. Smart. Rich. It was good to be a Rockefeller. Even in Hell.

"What did you do in New Guinea?" she asked in a breathy voice.

"I scouted for primordial art," he replied. "And did some fine dining." "The Dani tribe were his hosts," Lucifer explained, grinning at Rockefeller's tongue-in- cheek response. "They are headhunters. And cannibals."

Mardie's eyes went wide, but her mouth stayed shut.

Rockefeller handed the Devil a small metal dish with bullet slugs on it and a piece of paper with a description of the forensic results. Lucifer read the paper and looked up at Mili and Mardie.

"These bullets were recovered from the slaughter. Forensics folks have identified them as bullets fired from two different Russian-made automatic rifles, Kovrovskyi AEK-971s.

"So, the assassins were Russian?" Mardie guessed.

"Some seventy military forces around the world use those guns," Michael responded.

"Are those numbers skewed by any obvious factors?" Mili immediately asked. "Such as demographics?"

"Yes," Rockefeller responded. "The largest and most frequent purchasers are governments in Arab-speaking countries."

Mili nodded. Most Arab nations steered clear of dealings with the United States. Among their many reasons was a firm belief that the American government did not like Arabs. Or Persians. Or Asian Muslims. They were, of course, right. Plus, Russia not only made the best rifle of this type—even US Special Forces armed many of their clandestine troops with them—and the Russians actually supported Islamic nations whereas America tended to boycott them, ban their imports, and declare war on them. Had it been Arab shooters that had come looking for Dyn Suchland? Mili frowned. Dyn Suchland. What the hell kind of name was that?

✳ ✳ ✳

Lucifer led Mili into the dead soldier's flat. Mardie remained outside in the hallway. Two Samns bowed as Satan entered, then stayed to guard the open door. The apartment smelled of gore and the first stirrings of physical decay. The Devil opened all the windows while Mili observed Dyn Suchland's corpse.

The body was widening its print on the dead man's carpet. It had collapsed into a six- or seven-inch-thick pile of shredded flesh and organs, no longer differentiated by limbs or a head. It was simply a massive blob very much resembling raw hamburger, oatmeal, and miscellaneous filler ready to be shaped into patties.

Dear God, Mili thought. This shapeless protoplasm—the remains of a ferocious specimen of a man who had killed on his government's orders for three decades—was the final incarnation of Dyn Suchland. No human deserved such a fate.

Lucifer stood next to her. He started counting the slugs visible to the naked eye.

"One. Two. Three—"

"Please," Mili said, shushing her husband.

Satan shrugged his shoulders and went on counting silently.

Mili surveyed the ruins of Dyn Suchland. Did he have relatives? Did he have children? She looked around the sparsely furnished apartment. She didn't note any photographs of family or friends. The only picture on any wall was a formal portrait of the petty officer in his dress uniform. Hung on both sides of the picture were framed commendations he had won for bravery. How brave had he been when his killer had confronted him holding his rifle trained on his unarmed person? Mili suspected that Suchland had died as bravely as he had lived. She hoped he had earned one last commendation.

She saw that Lucifer was looking at her.

"Yes?" she asked.

"There are one hundred and nineteen slugs that I can see. Likely there are more buried in the goop. Given that all of the shots were fired before the first neighbors rushed in here, my guess is that the two shooters were able to run a full minute's worth of bullets through their AEK-971s. At a hundred rounds a minute that gives us a total of two hundred slugs."

"I'll take your word for it," Mili said sounding sour. "I'll have DNA samples taken, but there isn't a single other useful thing to be retrieved. I'm ready to go."

Mili walked out of the apartment.

Mardie was waiting in the hall.

"Any clues?" she asked.

Mili shook her head.

"Not one. Sterile flat. Pudding remains."

Mardie's face went pale.

"Anything taken?" she asked.

"Nothing to take," Mili answered.

"Anything that should have been?"

Mili studied her sister's face. Mardie was going somewhere with these questions. Mili had no idea where.

"The only thing even worth noting was that the victim had a portrait of himself on the wall in his navy uniform, next to framed commendations for bravery."

Mardie pondered that a moment.

"If this man was killed by someone with a personal score to settle, I'd think they'd have shot those down."

Son of a bitch, Mili thought excitedly. Mardie hadn't even gone into the apartment yet she'd just nailed the crime scene's most important clue. Dyn Suchland had been executed by professional assassins.

✳ ✳ ✳

Jim Elliot washed his hands with Lava soap. It cut through the grease stains. He'd been working on his 1956 Ford Mainline. It was a burgundy duplicate of the one he had totaled the night he'd graduated from high school. It had gone up in flames, but he had not. The navy had put someone else's body in the car whose remains had been identified as Elliot's. He went on to serve as a secret SEAL operative and then a high-ranking senior naval officer under a new identity. It was such a long time ago, now he had troubling remembering his real name.

He was bare-chested and he hated to look at his reflection in the mirror. His chest sagged and his arms were flaccid. He was bald and wore glasses. He stared at his sixty-year-old face. Bland. Vanilla. He'd never been handsome, but now he seemed featureless. Unnoticeable. He had turned into Gerald Ford.

As he scrubbed at his hands, he saw the reflections of two men appear behind him in the bathroom mirror. He turned to face them. They were young, dark-faced, dark-haired sons of Ishmael. He'd know them anywhere. He'd seen them. He'd followed them. He'd killed them. Over and over. And now two of them were in his home. One of them came close and rested the tip of his rifle on Elliot's chest.

The SEAL recognized it as the Muslim terrorists' weapon of choice, the Russian AEK-971. Some of his SEAL teams had armed themselves with those, leaving slugs that pointed fingers toward Arab assassins. But that never fooled those who found the dead bodies afterwards. They knew that Americans had left the calling cards.

"Take your damned gun off me," Elliot ordered the man whose rifle was touching his chest. The young man turned his face to look at his partner. The man nodded and the other pulled his rifle tip back from Elliot.

"What do you want?" Elliot demanded, fury in his voice.

"We only want you to remember a single deed," the apparent leader replied. "One deed from your catalog of atrocities. In one dark and forbidding place you called out to someone in Arabic. Do you remember?"

Elliot remembered. His target was in a second-floor room above him and his son had heard noise downstairs. The boy had peeked out of the door and looked down the stairs. Elliot saw his face in the shadows and whispered to him in Arabic.

"Khalid. It's me."

The boy stuck his head out the door to see who was calling him. Elliot shot him in the face.

"I remember," he said softly.

"We have come in the name of Khalid," the man said. Then he raised his rifle and shot Jim Elliot in the face.

*   *   *

Mili was back home when Lucifer called her. Mardie was on the porch smoking with Sriracha, Mili's sixteen-year-old son. He was a bright and funny boy, as beautiful as his father. Except while Lucifer cultivated a wavy blond mane down his shoulders, Sriracha shaved his head. It was a hip style among young men at the kibbutz, and Sriracha was at Ben-Yehuda High School taking art lessons.

He was also partnering with Agatha Christie up in Heaven to produce the first graphic novel about Mili and Mardie's earliest case, *The Wickett Sisters in Hell*. They had a lot of fans in Heaven and there were even re-enactments of their adventures. Go figure. Sriracha visited her a lot. He also liked to stop by his aunt Mardie's house down here who was having a long-term affair with Charlton Heston. She and Agatha Christie had become great chums, though the two women could hardly have been more different. Class and classless. Mili truly loved her sister, but Mardie was anything but genteel.

Mili answered her iPhone. Her husband's face showed on the mobile's screen.

"Hello, love," she said.

"Bad news," Lucifer told her.

Mili steeled herself.

Satan continued.

"Another Navy SEAL has been murdered."

"Same circumstances?"

"Yes. He was alone in his house when two assassins confronted him."

"The victim saw them?"

"They shot him in the face."

Dear God. Her secret fear as an inspector at Scotland Yard had always been that she would be shot in the face. Watching the perpetrator pull the trigger.

"I'll have Pfotenhauer pick you up," Satan told her. "The kids okay?"

Little Mardie was twenty-two and lived at the kibbutz. Sriracha split his time between Heaven and Hell. Jesus was ten and lived at home spending all of his time online. Not on games. On Oxford University college courses. And Union Theological Seminary graduate work.

"Mardie is with Sriracha," Mili answered, "and I'm sure she'll stay with him until I return."

"Love you," Lucifer said and was gone.

Suddenly Mili's mind was filled with questions. What happened after the SEAL had been shot? Had his body been disfigured with rifle blasts like the first murder victim? Had everything in the house been left untouched as before? Was there any trace of the assassins at the scene?

Mili fretted as she changed into black shorts and a taupe-colored short-sleeve blouse. She slipped her feet into her brown Birkenstock sandals. Then kicked them back off and pulled out some flats from her closet. She didn't mind blood on her shoes. She didn't like blood on her toes.

She went outside and asked Mardie if she would come in the house for a moment.

Sriracha waved at her and lit a new cigarette with the smoldering stub of his old one. She followed Mardie inside. Her sister was wearing 1950s-style pink pedal-pushers and a white halter top. She had had her body restored after Jack the Ripper had shot her, and her ass was pedal-pusher perfect. Having met God not all that long ago, Mili had learned that the Creator was a softie on female Hellion upgrades, and Lucifer was not afraid to ask.

Mardie sat down at the kitchen table.

"What's up?" she asked.

"Lucifer just called," Mili answered. "There's been a second murder."

"Oh, God," Mardie said.

"Another SEAL."

"So, the first was just the beginning," Mardie groaned.

Mili had not considered that, but how could it not be true? Assassins were loose in Hell and it was very likely they had a list of victims. Two down. How many to go before she could track the shooters down?

CHAPTER THREE

I am not going," Mardie said. There was a resolution to her voice that told Mili nothing was going to change her sister's mind.

"No problem," Mili assured her. "Pfot is on his way to pick me up and I was wondering if you would stay with the kids while I'm gone."

"Pour me another cup of coffee," Mardie responded, "and the answer is yes."

"Done."

Mili took her twin's empty cup and filled it with the last coffee in the pot.

"Are you on social media?" Mardie asked her.

"No. That's newfangled shite I don't need." Mili threw up her hands as if to say, who did? "Hell's wankers blogging away about nothing and posting new selfies round the clock."

"It's not *that* bad," Mardie protested.

Mili placed the coffee cup in front of Mardie.

"How many entries have you done today?"

"Four."

"And how many selfies?"

"Twelve."

"I rest my case."

"Go easy, Sis," Mardie complained. "People like to see each other's news."

"No," Mili snapped. "People like to see their *own* news. And their own idiotic photos."

"There's some of that," Mardie admitted. "But with ninety-six percent of all the damned souls down here subscribed to Hellbent, everything that gets uploaded is interesting. And fun. And harmless." Mardie poked a forefinger at Mili. "Never heard of subscribers killing anyone, have you?"

"You've got me there," Mili conceded.

"What I'm thinking," Mardie went on, "is that you should use social media to warn any and all former Navy SEALs down here about what's going on. It's obvious they're swimming around in the murderers' target pool, and as fast as the killers are moving, they've probably already picked out their next victim."

"There's huge merit in your idea," Mili told her sister. "As soon as I meet up with Lucifer, I'll work on getting that started."

"Also have Lu ask Pfot to check with his contacts in the demon network about what they might know. And encourage them to get the word out about the SEAL killer through their own blogs and their You-are-in-Hell-Tube accounts. Further, they might even know who's been buying the Russian guns the killers are using. I mean, how many AEK whatevers get sold down here?"

"Again, sterling advice," Mili told Mardie. "Anything else?"

Mardie nodded slowly.

"I'm not a fan of profiling. I sat on a plane once on the runway outside of Jerusalem's Ben-Gurion airport and watched as armed airport security guards removed every male passenger from the plane who looked like he was an Arab. I mean, not even a passport check first. Just taken off the plane.

"But..." Mardie said, "since the first Navy SEAL—and likely the second Navy SEAL as well—was shot to death by a Russian gun, it's not an exaggeration to suspect that the weapon was provided by an Arab country to men with a chip on their shoulders against American Navy special service men. SEALs who carried out missions on their sovereign turf and killed their family and friends."

Mili nodded. Food for thought. Or worse, fodder for thought. She looked at Mardie.

"I'll ask Lucifer to run checks on all of the Arab men in Hell. They have to be Christians though, even if in name only. Arab Muslims go to their own Heaven and Hell. But maybe a killer could turn up here. Avenging a Palestinian relative. Memorializing an Iraqi woman or child killed in one of the Gulf Wars."

Mardie nodded.

"What will Lu's folks look for?" she asked.

Mili shrugged helplessly.

"There is no way to tell them what to look for. But Satan's young team is pretty sharp. Hedge fund managers. They'll be able to spot an anomaly."

"Maybe," Mardie responded.

"Maybe," Mili agreed.

Mili saw Pfotenhauer pull up behind the house in the family's new white Tesla S coupe.

"Pfot's here. Call me if you get any more brainstorms."

"Count on it," Mardie promised. "And you can call me if you want the drugstore to send some Pepto Bismol over."

It was a crime scene deserving of a textbook entry. The victim had lived in a classic New England saltbox-style house in an upscale neighborhood of New Babylon. The house was painted red with a steeply pitched roof in front and a much longer sloping roof in back. Such houses had been popular in America since the earliest times, but Mili had never seen one before.

The Samn demons guarding the front door stepped aside and bowed as Lucifer and Mili entered the house. It was furnished with burgundy leather Chesterfields and wingback chairs upholstered in black-and-red plaids. Bookshelves lined the walls, and early American antique oil paintings hung anywhere a nail could be pounded into the wall.

Mili turned to Lucifer.

"This guy retired in style."

"Yes, he did," the Devil agreed. "His name was Jim Elliot. He left the navy after a thirty-year career. First as an active SEAL, and later as one of the special forces' senior officers. His final rank was full admiral."

Mili shook her head as she looked around at the beautiful home interior. The peacemakers of the world like Bishop Desmond Tutu or the Tibetan Dalai Lama had never been paid on a scale like the leaders who waged war. Admiral Elliot was a case in point. Gorgeous furniture. Expensive art. A beautiful house. Bloody hands.

"Elliot's body is in one of the upstairs bathrooms," Lucifer told Mili.

He led her up the stairs and paused on the second floor to look down a long hall. Rooms were located on both sides. The bathroom they were looking for was through a doorway with a blood-soaked carpet mat outside. They looked inside. Straight ahead was a cabinet with a mirror and a recessed sink. To the left was a white upright bathtub with lion claw feet. Inside of it were the piled up remains of the admiral.

An iron pipe with faucets hung above the tub. Fastened to the pipe was a pair of handcuffs holding hands and arms that had been shot with bullets beyond count. The admiral's torso had ripped free at the shoulders and dropped into the tub. His body had been shot into a heap of broken bones, raw muscles, torn skin, and blood. It looked like it had been spewed from a leviathan that had failed to digest it.

Mili felt a rise in her stomach, and for the first time in her career she turned away from a crime scene. She went back into the hall and sat down in a straight-back Chippendale chair. Lucifer came out and knelt. He took one of her hands. No one spoke, and in a few moments Mili appeared to be recovering. The Devil spoke gently to his wife.

"Is there any reason to stay?" he asked.

Mili shook her head. She stood, and still holding her husband's hand she walked down the hall, descended the stairs, and left the house. She was still overwhelmed. This unholy act was the most brutal murder she had ever witnessed. As bad and worse than the murder of the first Navy SEAL. Elliot had been hung by his wrists above his own bathtub and had not only been shot to death, but to oblivion. Dear God. It made Jack the Ripper's work look like amateurish. Who were these murderous animals? And how many more SEALs did they plan to destroy?

She and Lucifer walked toward the Tesla. Mili talked to her husband before they got in the car.

"Mardie and I think that you should advise any Navy SEALs down here about what is happening. Also, it wouldn't hurt to have your demons get the word out that you are interested in learning who might have recently bought or sold Russian AEK-971s."

Satan nodded.

"Consider both actions underway," he replied. "I'll have Rockefeller get word out to the surviving SEALs to prep themselves for an attack. If anyone can defend themselves against vengeance it's them. I will personally check with demons connected to the gun trade down here about the Russian rifles."

"The *illegal* gun trade down here," Mili reminded him.

"Of course," the Devil said in a huff. "Just because guns have been smuggled down here doesn't mean I approve. The whole trade is outlawed."

Right, darling, Mili thought. But you never make any effort to completely shut down the smugglers, do you? Money was changing hands somewhere. And she suspected that Lucifer's were on the receiving end. Was her husband avaricious or greedy? Perhaps not. But for an Archangel who was already rich beyond belief, he certainly did seem to be involved wherever the money was.

"Coming home for dinner?" Mili asked him as they got in the car. Pfotenhauer was dropping Satan off at his office and taking Mili home.

"Sure," the Devil replied. "Think I can get my action items done this afternoon. I'll try to be home by seven. How would that be?"

"Perfect. We'll have a glass of Prosecco and I'll cook."

"Nice," Lucifer said. "Make sure to have a *lot* of Prosecco."

Mili looked at her husband, understanding without having to ask. "You got it."

Lucifer gave Mili a peck on the cheek and got out in front of his downtown office building.

"Bye, Doll," he told Mili.

"Ciao, Bello," she said and smiled.

"Any stops on the way home, Mrs. Mili?" Pfotenhauer inquired as he pulled the car away from the curb. "Sriracha asked if I would bring him home some cigarettes. Is that permissible?"

"Sure. What is that character smoking these days? He probably graduated from American Spirits long ago."

"Ay. That he did," Pfot replied. He was dressed in a suit, white shirt, and tie. Always dapper. Always professional. "He asked me for a dozen cartons of unfiltered Pall Malls."

"Pall Malls? Do cigarettes get any stronger than that?"

"They do indeed, Mrs. Mili. French Gauloise cigarettes come in ascending stages of ferocity. I smoked them as a young lad."

"Until you wised up?"

"No. Until I switched to smoking whatever fags my boss extorted from his London clients."

Paul Pfotenhauer had been a mob boss's chauffeur for most of his adult life and was a serious stoolie for Mili when she worked at the Yard. He was Lucifer's driver now and took his family wherever they needed or wanted to be. He was eighty and somewhat off-putting to look at with a thin bony face and scant white hair. But it hadn't stopped him from being a lothario with the seventy-plus ladies at the kibbutz. He had charm, personality, and a tadger that just didn't quit. Mili loved and admired Pfot.

"Pfot," Mili went on. "Have any of your demon connections mentioned the new string of murders that are occurring down here?"

"Yes, ma'am. The wires, so to speak, are burning up with gossip about the two military men who have been killed."

"What kind of gossip?" Mili asked.

"It's known that two American Navy SEALs have been killed and their bodies mutilated by gunfire. Rumors are abounding that the shooters are Arabs armed with Russian automatic rifles."

"That's all on target," Mili confirmed.

"There is some talk of the killers being with Russian special forces. In part because the active gun arms dealers down here agree that no Russian weapons have been imported, ordered, or purchased in Hell. Seems then that the shooters must have somehow *entered* Hell carrying their choice of firepower, versus procuring their weapons down here."

"They're from Earth then?" Mili asked.

"Where else?" Pfot asked rhetorically. "Arabs tracking down and killing US military assassins with some kind of nefarious history with their country, or family, or neighbors. And they're not just *killing* the SEALs, but are wreaking havoc on their dead bodies. Out-of-control rage unleashed. Fury that bubbled for a long time and is now bubbling over."

"The gossips are pretty accurate," Mili admitted. "Firearms can be brought in through a wormhole and have been. And on that point, dear boy, would it be possible for you to ferret out whether some fallen angel is helping the assassins enter Hell?"

"I can certainly prod a devil butt here and there," Pfot answered. "But helping the assassins is a betrayal few devils would risk. It's not only a sellout of Hell's residents, but it goes directly against Master Lucifer as well."

"Please proceed," Mili said. "And with haste. I can't say why, but my feeling is that the killings have only just started. And *someone* has to be telling them exactly where the victims reside. I would like to limit the assassins' success, Pfot. And the sooner the better."

"I will get on it ASAP, ma'am. With a bit of luck, I'll have something today."

"Thank you, Pfot. Lucifer is also beating the bushes looking for suspect gun smugglers. And he has his chief assistant trying to warn any SEALs living down here as to what's going down."

"That's good," Pfot replied. "Might wind up saving their lives."

"From your lips to God's ears," Mili wished.

"Yep," Pfot said. "Let's just hope he's not absorbed in some new television show."

✳ ✳ ✳

Lucifer did indeed make it home in time for family dinner, and Mardie was invited to stay for supper as well. Mili had prepared pork chops, scalloped potatoes, Brussel sprouts, and brown-and-serve rolls. Everyone ate everything, including Jesus the vegetarian, who ate a pork chop because it was from an animal that was a vegetarian. The adults enjoyed endless glasses of Prosecco that Mili had picked up at Hells Bells when she had stopped to buy Sriracha's Pall Malls.

Dinner conversation was light and entertaining. A refreshing diversion from the confusion and violence that had descended on Hell. Sriracha talked about the momentum he was drawing into his sequential cartoon art as he discussed progress on his first graphic novel *The Wickett Sisters in Hell*. Jesus talked about the discoveries of the royal tombs of Ur by Leonard Woolley in the 1920s. He had been delighted when Aunt Mardie told him that Max Mallowan—Agatha Christie's husband—was Woolley's good friend and archaeological partner.

Near the end of the meal, Lucifer took a call on his mobile phone. He stepped out of the kitchen while the dinner conversations continued. He returned a few minutes later and sat down for coffee and dessert. He didn't speak about the call, but he had a very pleased expression on his face. When several conversations were going on at the same time, he leaned over and whispered in Mili's ear. Two assassins. Both gunned down by a SEAL waiting for them.

Mili sighed with relief. Then she poured tea for Mardie, Lucifer, and herself, and passed out heaping bowls of vanilla ice cream covered with chocolate-dipped strawberries. Mardie and Lucifer passed on dessert. She didn't. She ate hers. And then she ate theirs.

CHAPTER FOUR

Captain Ron Bull was in his condo, dressed in khaki pants, an olive T-shirt, and black short-top boots. He was eating saltine crackers spread with humus. It was a snack that he'd acquired a taste for during his SEAL days in the Middle East. There wasn't a country in that geography that had not buried men he had killed. Bad men. At least he believed so. His country had identified them as enemies and he had terminated their lives as ordered. He'd also done an occasion mission farther east. The Philippines, Indonesia, and Pakistan.

He'd gotten the emergency warning from Satan's headquarters that all Navy SEALs in Hell should prepare to repel assassins who had ambushed two SEALs in their homes and were expected to target more. Bull always had his Israeli Uzi close by. He had been on alert during his entire Navy career, waiting for someone to come looking for him. He had died of natural causes a year ago and found himself down here. Even as he'd always been prepared to defend his life before he died, he was mentally and emotionally prepared to defend it now. Tonight. Tomorrow. Whenever. He moved the Uzi to his lap. Which was good. Turned out it was tonight.

There was no warning. His front door was suddenly broken down. He instantly spun on the sofa, firing the Uzi at two men rushing into his home. He shot them dead. No one had ever survived a dozen shots from his pet. He got up and looked at the men. They were dressed in black jeans, plain black T-shirts, and black lightweight jackets. They both had black hair. Black whiskers. Black eyes staring at his ceiling. Clearly Arabs. And while he did not consider himself an expert on the nuances of Arab physiognomy, his history of murdering Arab people in one particular locale led him to guess that both men were Saudis. Good. He hated Saudis.

They were phony bastards who played the United States for all it was worth. Business deals. Jet fighters. Diplomatic immunity. All the while screwing Americans with OPAC gouging and billions of dollars funneled to anti-American terrorists worldwide. Fuckers. If he had his way he'd kill every damn man, woman, and kid in that Islamic shithole. No. He'd spare the women. They had just finally been allowed to drive. They could kill each other off on the highways.

Bull bent down and picked up one of the killers' weapons. A Russian AEK-971. He loved that gun. Too damn big for him to carry around, but if worse had come to worse, he took some pleasure knowing that he would have been taken out by a 971. He held it in his hand. Aimed it at the open door. He decided that he'd hide this rifle and claim that the intruders had only brought one weapon.

He found extra magazines in the inner pockets of both men's jackets and took them. Bull glanced one more time at the faces of the two dead men. One looked very familiar, but he couldn't place where he might have seen him. With swift kicks of his boot, he broke the jaws of both Arab operatives and hummed "Anchors Aweigh" while he hid his treasures. Then he called the 24/7 number listed on the terrorist warning he'd received and shared the good news.

✳ ✳ ✳

Drinking one last cup of breakfast tea with Mili at the kitchen table, Lucifer shared what he knew about the incident at Captain Ronald Bull's condominium. The SEAL's home had been forcibly entered by two armed assailants. But Bull was prepared for them thanks to the emergency bulletin Michael Rockefeller had issued under the Devil's name. One of the intruders was armed and the other apparently came along as muscle. Bull had shot both of them using an Israeli Uzi.

He told the two Samns who rushed to his home after his phone call that he had bought the automatic weapon when he had first come to Hell. One of the Samns asked if he knew that possessing any gun was illegal in Hell. Bull told him he didn't give a fuck. If the navy man had known more about Samn tempers he might have lightened up a bit. The Samn he spoke to warned him that a second rude remark would get his arms pulled off. The captain took it seriously and became a model of respect.

Pictures and fingerprints of the two dead assassins were emailed to Satan's headquarters.

There was nothing on file. Michael had taken the liberty of forwarding the information to the demon network requesting IDs on the men from Earth when and if doable. He had no doubt that the men were Arabs from somewhere there, but they might be operating under the radar on Earth just as effectively as they were doing down here.

"It's not over," Mili remarked. "Three diverse targets rule out a blood vendetta. Which suggests that the victims were targeted *precisely* because they had served as SEALs. So, what is the mastermind's criteria? Kill *all* the SEALs in Hell? Why not? One individual with the will and the means could send endless young killers down here to pursue a jihad against the nistrani who they believe had violated Arab soil with blood and death."

"Nistrani?" Lucifer asked puzzled.

"It's an Islamic term for Europeans that dates back to the time when the Arabs encountered the knights of the First Crusade. Its current use is pejorative."

"Meaning that it's evolved into a derogatory term?" Satan asked.

"Yes. It means uncircumcised Christian."

"Men?" Lucifer asked frowning.

"Yes," Mili told him. "Unless you know something that I don't."

The Devil's face flushed and he shook his head.

✳ ✳ ✳

Mili was talking on the phone with Mardie, still sitting at the kitchen table. Lucifer had left for the office. Sriracha and Jesus were still asleep. Mili was still in her terrycloth bathrobe and she could see on her phone monitor that Mardie was in her nightgown. Mili had filled her sister in on Ron Bull's successful takedown of the two Arab assassins.

"I have an appointment to visit Bull at his home this afternoon," Mili said. "I want you to come along."

"Meet and greet the hero?" Mardie asked.

"Something like that. At least this SEAL is alive to talk about the attack."

"Good on him. I prefer a man who still has his blood and guts tucked *inside* his skin."

Mili laughed and then felt a little ashamed. She had seen two men rendered into pulp for serving their country.

"Pfot will swing by in an hour," Mili finished and pressed *Off*.

✳ ✳ ✳

Mardie was waiting on her porch when Pfot pulled up with Mili. He opened the passenger door for Mardie and greeted her happily.

"Ms. Mardie, how are you?"

"I am well, Pfot, thank you," she replied, getting into the Tesla's back seat. "And how are you?"

"Wonderful, thank you."

34

Mardie patted Mili's hand as she sat.

Pfot closed the door, circled round the car, and got in the driver's seat. He had the address where Mili wanted to go. It was in a nice high-rise condominium unit in downtown New Babylon. He started the car and left Mardie's house behind.

Mardie wore a sundress with a dandelion print and yellow sandals. Mili wore a dark blue skirt and a white shell with a high scoop neck.

"So, who is this guy we're meeting?" Mardie asked.

"Captain Ronald Bull," Mili answered. "Twenty years in the United States Navy SEALs, and then another twenty years running his own private security agency. Died a year ago of a cardiac infarction."

"Booze and smokes?"

"No. He was running on a treadmill and tore an artery in his heart."

"Oh, God."

"Bull shot two assassins when they broke into his condo," she continued. "They were carted to the hospital morgue last night. There are no IDs or files on either one of them down here. One of Lucifer's assistants forwarded their pictures and fingerprints to the demon network. I believe that the men are from Earth. Probably the Mideast. Right now, though, they're just anonymous guests at the morgue.

"My instincts tell me that they were hired help," Mili continued. "Contracted by some individual or group on Earth to exterminate American special forces personnel in Hell. All of the victims have been Navy SEALs who at some point in their careers carried out assignments in Arab countries. Two of the SEALs are dead. I have no reason to think that they will be the only ones. I am waiting now for the other shoe to fall and for the murders to resume."

Mardie thought about that a moment. Mili's criteria for potential victims was broad. American secret operations sailors with a history of activity in the Arab world. But it was also narrow in that the assassins were tracking only those individuals. She looked at Mili.

"Have you checked to see whether or not Navy SEALs are being targeted on Earth? Might tell us about the breadth of this hunt."

"That's brilliant, Sis!" was Mili's enthusiastic response. "When we finish with Captain Bull, I'll call Lucifer." Mili paused and looked her twin in the eyes. "I miss you when I have to do the Scotland Yard thing without you."

"I am sorry, Mili. I truly am," Mardie answered. "I want to be by you in every situation. But I do much better when a dead person is not present."

Pfot pulled into a visitor's parking spot and Mili and Mardie took a high-speed elevator to Bull's sixteenth-story condo. Mili reflected on the fact that not many years ago not a single elevator in Hell worked. Living high up had been only for the fit. Now, both terrorists and detective ladies could get up to the top. No problem.

Mili knocked on Bull's door. It was splintered along the inside edge and filled with bullet holes. There was no peephole. She figured Bull's new door would have one. A strong male voice came from behind the door.

"Identify yourself."

"Milicent Morningstar and my sister Mardie Wickett."

The door opened no more than an inch. The short barrel of an automatic Uzi was pushed out of the opening. Then inch by inch, the door opened by some three inches. A man's eye appeared from behind the door. Then it swung open and Ron Bull stood before them. He was tall and solid. Six foot, maybe one hundred and ninety pounds. He was wearing khaki pants and an olive T-shirt. His face was lined and his salt-and-pepper hair was cut shot. A smile slowly crossed his lips.

"Ladies, you are lovely," he said, taking a long moment to eye each one top to bottom. "But today is not my birthday."

"Beg pardon?" Mili responded.

"I didn't order any strippers," Bull answered.

Mili got angry, but Mardie laughed out loud.

"You've got some balls, you old bugger," she told Bull. "You know damn well who we are." Bull grinned and listened. "What you may not know is that this woman is Lucifer's wife, and if you piss her off, you'll have all the demons in Hell on your ass."

Bull's grin disappeared. Glints of fear shown in his eyes. Something Mardie thought was probably pretty rare.

"Forgive me, Mrs. Morningstar, and you, too, Ms. Wickett," Bull said hastily. "My bad manners are only exceeded by my poor judgment. Please come in." He stepped aside and pointed at the rug inside the apartment. "Be alert where you step. Haven't got everything replaced since yesterday's incident."

"Which you handled masterfully," Mili told him and stepped over the blood-soaked carpet. Mardie followed. Bull shut the door.

"No locks?" Mardie asked surprised.

"No," Bull answered. "Never thought I needed them down here. The assholes who broke in could have just opened the door and I never would have heard them come in."

"Apparently both you and they were old-fashioned types," Mardie commented.

Bull chuckled.

"Saved *my* fuckin' neck," he told her.

He asked the ladies to sit. His living room was furnished with a white leather sofa and white overstuffed leather chairs, powder blue wall-to-wall carpet, and several expensive framed prints of naked women by Patrick Nagel. Bull's windows had no curtains and offered stunning views of the city. Mili and Mardie sat on the sofa and the captain took a chair.

Mardie sat on something. She reached down and retrieved a bullet casing.

"Guilty," Bull told her. "Sorry I missed that. I was sitting there when I greeted my visitors."

Mardie chuckled and dropped the spent shell in her clutch.

"Would you tell us what happened here yesterday?" Mili asked. "No detail is unimportant."

Captain Bull told his story. It was thorough but short, finishing with ambulances arriving and paramedics taking out the dead men in black zip-up bags.

"I know you have likely thought about what happened over and over since it occurred," Mili said when the SEAL was done. "Do you have any idea why you were targeted?"

"No," Bull answered. "Since there have been other attacks on SEALs before this one, I have to think that I have somehow been shuffled into a deck of targets along with other SEALs who served in Arab locations. Who wants us dead is a mystery. And with more than a billion Arabs in the world, there's a lot of candidates."

Mili and Mardie sat silently. Suddenly Ron Bull had another comment.

"One of the assassin's faces looked familiar. Thought maybe I'd seen him in Saudi Arabia before I killed him. You might check to see if there are two old bullet wounds in one of the corpse's sternums."

"So, the face you thought you recognized," Mardie asked, "belonged to a man you had already killed?"

"Yes."

"And he entered here as a dead man?"

Bull stared at Mardie for a long moment.

"Yep," he finally replied. "And he left here as a dead man."

Mili filed that away for future thought. It was rather unlikely that a man Bull had killed in Saudi Arabia had come back from the dead to get even. Yesterday's assassin was a look-alike, or maybe even a relative of the murdered Arab. The latter possibility could wind up being a motive if provable. But the Saudi connection was intriguing. Though the United States chose to ignore Saudi Arabian sponsored terrorism against its neighbors in the Arab world, the British secret service estimated that the Saudis spent billions of dollars and launched hundreds of clandestine missions every year. Almost as big a terrorist nation as America.

Bull kept eyeing Mardie and then looking up at a Nagel print on his wall of a large-busted woman with hungry eyes. When Mili and Mardie rose to go, he had a last comment for Mardie.

"Do you see that print?" he asked and pointed at the one he had been studying. "I think you might have modeled for it."

Mardie smiled, flattered.

"Would you mind," Bull continued, "taking off your clothes so I can see for myself?"

CHAPTER FIVE

Pfotenhauer took Mili and Mardie to the city morgue located in New Babylon's only hospital. They identified themselves and received permission from the hospital administrator to examine the bodies of the two dead assassins chilling in the morgue. Mili remembered when young people used to tell each another to chill out. She doubted that they had the big chill in mind. Doubted too, that the two Arab men who broke into Ron Bull's apartment suspected for a moment that the following morning they'd be lying dead in vinyl bags on morgue gurneys.

As they were being escorted by a security guard, Mili turned to Mardie.

"Sure you're okay with this?" she asked.

Mardie nodded.

"If I have to see a dead body, I prefer it to be cleaned up and stored somewhere proper, not still lying around in its death throes."

"Death throes?" Mili asked.

"Blood, organs, bones, vomit, and waste."

Mili frowned.

"No one likes that," she told her sister. "These cadavers will be presentable."

Mardie followed Mili inside the morgue after the guard unlocked the door. It was a small, very cold room with white tile walls and white tile floors. There was a metal sink and a small table with autopsy tools. There were two gurneys on wheels in the center of the room, each holding a black body bag.

Mili pulled down the zipper on the first bag. The young, thin face of a dark-haired, dark-skinned man lay inside. His eyes were closed and his face was whole. His shoulders, chest, and abdomen, however, were covered with bullet holes. Mili leaned down and looked at the man's chest. All of the wounds penetrating his sternum were new. There were no scars.

The second man was equally riddled with bullet holes, but between his mocha-colored nipples two small scars marked his skin. Each one was maybe an inch long. They were close to one another. Both were bullet wounds that would have pierced the bone and penetrated the man's heart.

So, Captain Bull had remembered his victim's face accurately. And that he'd put two bullets in his chest once upon a time. Mili stared at the corpse. If Bull was indeed correct that he had killed this man, then somehow the Arab had received a new life. And a new assignment. Finding and killing Ron Bull.

Mili shook her head slightly. God that sounded corny. Bull's comments could be mistaken. This man could also be another avenging warrior that some other Ron Bull had stopped with two slugs to the heart. Both men had been fingerprinted and she expected Lucifer or Pfotenhauer—both of whom had accessed the vast and well-informed demon network—to identify these assassins from earthly existences.

Mardie watched while her sister examined chests and torsos, heads and faces. She noted that both of the deceased had been nice-looking young men. Was there a woman waiting for either one of them? Fearing the worst? Worrying yet again that her man had embarked on an assignment that would cost him his life?

Fuck these boys, Mardie thought. They had chosen their task and they had earned their pay. She had no sympathy for them. Any more than she would have any concerns if it would have been Navy SEAL Ron Bull lying here. You got what you had coming.

"Where to, ladies?" Pfotenhauer asked when Mili and Mardie had exited the morgue. Mili looked at her sister.

"Are you up for a falafel?"

"*Arab* food?" Mardie asked surprised, considering she and Mili had just been viewing dead Arabs.

"Yes. A Palestinian Christian runs a great little place only a few blocks from here. Lucifer and I eat there a lot. Good food and I wouldn't mind asking the owner Wasim some questions about what makes a vendetta so important to an Arab."

"You mean a Muslim?" Mardie asked.

"No. Muslim and Arab are not one and the same. Islam teaches honor and the struggle to do what is right. Vengeance is not Muslim. It was never taught or sanctioned by Muhammad. It is, however, a traditional *Arab* value. I want to ask Wasim how long an Arab can bear a grudge. And how long they should seek to fulfill its obligations."

Mardie scowled.

"You're going to have that conversation while we eat?"

Mili pursed her lips and thought for a moment.

"How about you and Pfot relax and have lunch together, and I'll ask Wasim to join me at a separate table."

"Okay," Mardie replied.

"You, Pfot?" Mili asked.

"It would be an honor to dine with Ms. Mardie," he replied humbly.

"It will be fun, Pfot," Mardie declared. "You can regale me with stories of your sex life."

Pfotenhauer blushed radish red and kept silent.

"It's okay to pass on that," Mili told him. "Just don't allow Mardie to share hers."

Pfot smiled, but he was clearly ready to move on from this subject.

"We're heading to the Falafel House on Blaney," Mili said, getting in the car. "Do you know where that is?"

Pfot shut her door and watched Mardie get in the back seat and close hers. He got in front and answered Mili.

"Yes, I do ma'am. I'll have you there in five minutes."

Mili looked at her sister.

"You were naughty to Pfot," she said and shook her finger.

"Ha!" Mardie snorted. "The man has half the widows at the kibbutz waiting for his visits. Don't naughty me. I was just curious."

Pfot pulled into a street parking spot and he, Mili, and Mardie walked into the Falafel House, an Arab restaurant occupying a building that looked like a big red barn and had once offered farm fresh breakfasts. That had been back in the day when nothing in Hell was fresh. It had gone out of business fairly quickly.

The restaurant had booths and tables. Wasim himself personally welcomed everyone. He was a middle-aged man with a bald head ringed with white fringe, a large belly, sparkling brown eyes, and a welcoming smile. He took them to a corner booth. Mardie and Pfotenhauer sat, and Mili asked if she could speak to Wasim alone for a few minutes. He waved toward the kitchen and a young man came out immediately to serve the newcomers. Wasim ordered a falafel for Mili and invited her to sit at a table across the room from Mardie and Pfot.

"Dear Mrs. Morningstar," he began. "I am so honored to have you dine once again in my establishment." Wasim was wearing black slacks and a long-sleeve white shirt. Dressed like an Israeli. Or maybe the Israeli's were dressed like Arabs. Either way, someone was going to be unhappy with the comparison.

"Thank you, Wasim," Mili answered. "How are you and how is your family?"

"Kalila is well, and the two boys have high-tech jobs in Tel-Aviv."

"But they're still living in Gaza?"

"Yes, and they're still alive, God be praised."

Mili nodded.

"Wasim, have you heard about the murders in Hell this week?"

"Yes, I have. Such news always saddens me. This is no place for old vendettas."

"Then you know that Arab assassins killed two discharged American Navy personnel, and that they or other attackers were killed when they attacked a third SEAL?"

"Yes," Wasim answered and shook his head sadly. "I employ two very nice demons who bus and wash dishes here. According to them, the shooters were indeed Arabs, but not from down here. The gossip is that they came from Earth and tracked their victims down in Hell."

"Any word on why the SEALs were singled out?"

"Nothing specific, but there is general agreement that the murdered sailors were part of a large number of navy special forces down here who carried out secret missions in Arab countries."

"So, no eye for an eye, or tooth for a tooth retaliation against specific men for specific killings?"

"It doesn't appear so. The men who were attacked were deemed guilty of crimes against Arab citizens and were punished. Members of a broad jihad to punish military assassins who murdered men, women, and children on the orders of their government."

"Have you heard that the SEAL victims were not just shot, but shot hundreds of times?"

"Yes," Wasim answered, speaking softly. "That kind of madness is beyond my ken. I have never heard of such mutilation before. To what purpose?"

Wasim's server brought Mili a foil-wrapped falafel and set two bottles of sauce on the table for her. Tahini and hot sauce.

"Let me fetch some iced tea for us," Wasim told Mili. "We shall talk of less brutal things while you dine. Please start your lunch."

Mili did. And while she appreciated her host's kind offer to move on to other topics besides the slaughter going on down here, she had a lot more to ask him on that subject. Besides, she could eat her lunch without being bothered in the slightest by talk of murder and mayhem. Thanks to her years at Scotland Yard, she could eat even in the company of dead men. They never interrupted. And they told no tales as the cliché went. They also didn't ask to share your food.

* * *

At home that night Mili and Lucifer spoke about a possible jihad against the SEALs. Information from the demon network had yielded no clues concerning specific identities of the Arab assassins.

"They are not readily identifiable," Lucifer told Mili. "Undercover agents, perhaps."

"Like Jim Elliot?" Mardie asked. "A man who did not officially exist, leaving him free to do terrible untraceable things for his controller."

"These terrorists probably believe that their violent deeds are for their country, too."

"A familiar refrain, no?" was Mili's reaction. "I killed the Saudi family because my platoon leader said they were harboring rebels against the republic. I killed the Navy SEAL because my leader told me he was a murderer of Arab people."

"I understand," Satan replied. "Everyone finds a way to commit murder. And then excuse it."

* * *

Friday night poker had been a tradition for the three men who'd served together as SEALs and had been sent off to Hell together by a Libyan pipe bomb tossed into their sleeping quarters. By the twelve-year-old boy who'd polished their boots and bummed their American cigarettes.

Greg Smith, Forey Walter, and Steve Lightbody were enjoying themselves in Steve's small apartment. Pretzels, cocktail onions, dill pickles, and a bowl full of Twinkies sat on one side of the kitchen table next to a metal tub full of Budweiser canned beer on ice. The men sat on the other side of the table playing cards, each man's weapon of choice resting on his lap, pants pockets stuffed with extra rounds.

Two of the former SEALs—Smith and Walter—nestled Uzi's. The weight of the automatics pressed down on their penises. It felt good. So good, in fact, the only way to top it would be to rest the guns on their naked dicks. Lightbody carried a Marine Corps M39 Enhanced Marksman Rifle on his lap. It was only a semi-automatic rifle, but unlike the Uzi, it had a deadly range of more than 850 yards and a maximum accuracy range of 4,000 yards. Uzis blasted the living shit out of anything close up. The Marksman could take out a towel-head drinking Turkish coffee in front of a cafe two miles away.

It was an evening of laughter and fellowship, but different than other poker nights they'd shared. All three soldiers kept their eyes and ears tuned to the front door of Lightbody's apartment. Their watchfulness had been necessitated by Satan's warning that terrorists had slain two Navy SEALs and had attacked another SEAL who'd managed to turn the tables on them and shot them down. Lucifer believed that additional assassins would likely follow these first attackers.

In the day, the three SEALs had taken out targets in and around Riyadh, Baghdad, and Islamabad. Arabs. Saudi Arabs. Saudi Muslim Arabs. Saudi Sunni Muslim Arabs. Saudi Salafi Sunni Muslim Arabs. Hearing that Saudi bastards were down here in Hell made all three of the men earnestly desire that some of those assholes would be looking for them. Turned out some of them were.

The door to Lightbody's apartment burst open, but before anyone could enter, all three SEALs fired their weapons at whoever had crashed it in. There was no return fire. The three men were up and out the door in pursuit of trespassers they could hear fleeing down the fire stairs at the end of the apartment hall. The SEALs raced down the steps and pushed open the door at the bottom. Gunfire met their exit and a spray of bullets caught Greg Smith. He fell with the top of his head blown off.

Walter and Lightbody crawled outside and returned fire. The men shooting at them stopped firing and ran for their lives. The two SEALs were instantly on their feet running after them. Off and on, barrages of weapon fire were exchanged. Lightbody called in the SEALs' location to Satan's hotline and within five minutes other SEALs from the neighborhood had joined in the conflict. Some ran with Walter and Lightbody in hot pursuit, and others positioned themselves in front of the fleeing assassins. Invisible in the dark, they were waiting for the approaching killers.

The conflict raged through the night as hundreds of rounds were fired back and forth. Two times the escaping shooters broke through the SEALs' lines, killing men as they fled. The assassins were not eliminated until daylight the next morning, and in the end, six SEALs gave their lives to take out the two jihadists.

Not only did Smith die, but so did Walter and Lightbody. They were A.J. Squared Away SEALs who had pulled their weight. Each SEAL took out one of the Saudi Salafi Sunni Muslim Arabs before succumbing. They died happy men.

CHAPTER SIX

There were now eleven dead men in the hospital morgue. Two doctors and two attendants had been assigned temporary duty to manage the number of slain men piled up on the twin gurneys. Today, the city had been quiet so far. Had perhaps the thwarted wave of new assassins exhausted the number of young men sent to murder and die?

The SEALs who had been killed yesterday had had their identities confirmed. They served together for their entire twenty-year careers in the navy, completing some one hundred and seventy successful missions. While they had been assigned targets in various countries, the majority of their operations had been in the Mideast and in Saudi Arabia specifically.

This information had been provided from the records of the United States Navy at Lucifer's request. He had close ties to many of its most senior officers. Close ties that had to do with having sold their souls to the Devil. Mili remembered when she had made fun of Satan back when for engaging in such spooky business. But every time he pulled off a coup like this one, she apologized again. He was always gracious, but he didn't tell her to stop.

Mili opened the body bags and examined the dead men. They were empty of any sign of life. She had never figured out exactly what a soul, or *the* soul was. It was not the body. Earthly bodies were replaced by Heavenly or Hellion bodies. And those could be replicated if necessary. Both she and Mardie had been given replacement Hellion bodies.

Neither did the soul seem to be a so-called spark of life, either. It was closer to a feeling of immediate presence. A breath of life. A sustaining sangfroid. Temporary. Then gone. Whatever it was, she could tell that it was no longer present in the men in the morgue she was examining. Their bodies had been abandoned by their souls. They were not men anymore. They were refuse. Destined for the incinerator.

✳ ✳ ✳

Afterwards, Mili and Mardie were at Mili's home drinking tea and appreciating that the fighting in Hell had ceased for now.

Mardie tapped Mili on the shoulder.

"What are you thinking about?" she asked.

Mili looked at her.

"I feel a bit melancholy," she replied. "So much death. So many lives ended. And for what? Revenge? Settling a score? Once-vital men—on both sides of the conflict—invested in death and got paid its inevitable dividends."

"There's going to be more," Mardie said. "It's quiet now, and no one accomplished anything. Nothing's been resolved. So, it's only a matter of time before the shooting starts up again."

Mili looked sad and defeated.

"I am afraid that you are right. How ugly is that?"

"Ugly, and about to get uglier," Mardie told her. "I went out to have a smoke and visited with Pfot. He says that the demon network is on fire with gossip."

Mili arched an eyebrow. She hated demons for the malicious and dishonest activities they were involved in. But their gossip always had a ring of truth to it, and usually made the rounds of their networks before anyone else really had a clue as to what was going on. What were they hearing now?

"What kind of gossip?" she asked.

"Diverse and unpleasant possibilities," her twin responded. "Lucifer has received an offer from the US Navy to deploy twenty-five hundred active SEALs supported by an additional twenty-five hundred Marines. *Down here*."

Mili was stunned.

"Down here? That sounds like we're declaring war."

"As good as," Mardie agreed. "The navy wants to locate and exterminate the assassins who are determined to take out the SEALs in Hell."

"Did Pfot say whether the demons knew how Lu reacted?"

"He was appreciative of the offer, but cool to the idea. What he asked for instead was that the US provide all information from the world's databases on known or suspected Arab terrorists, their families, and their acquaintances."

Mili held up her hand.

"Stop, please. Do you mean he requested the information possessed on America's government and military databases?"

"Lucifer apparently said the *world's* databases." Mardie looked dismayed at her sister's naivete. "Any US spy capability that can hack into and record personal mobile phone conversations of the world's top leaders would have access to *any* nation's information on terrorists and their organizations."

"Good point," Mili told her sister. "And such data would be a goldmine of clues…" Mili stopped speaking.

Mardie was alarmed.

"What?" she demanded. "Finish your sentence."

"Unless the organizers of this jihad against the SEALs are so well-concealed and protected by the highest circles of power and wealth that no one outside of the terrorist cell knows about it."

"Meaning?" Mardie pressed.

"The Saudis are backing it," Mili answered.

"The Saudi government?"

Mili's face turned grim.

"The Saudi royals."

✳ ✳ ✳

Lucifer was sitting behind his desk. He had surrounded himself with Shapeshifter demons who primarily worked on Earth. They controlled hundreds of billions of dollars invested in commercial big business, precious metals including bitcoin, venture banking, and where helpful, strategic internet hacking and espionage. They were enormously rich and completely corrupt, wheeling and dealing with the Kochs, Carlos Helu, Jack Ma, Bernard Arault, Amancia Ortega, and the like.

The Shapeshifters never revealed who they were or who they worked with—only meeting with the Devil when the occasion demanded—but their impact on world finance and global economic wealth was virtually unlimited. They never dealt with government figures—even powerful ones like Donald Trump or Vladimir Putin. The real power in the world lay with the figures who controlled its money.

Satan looked at the dozen Shapeshifters seated on the other side of his desk. Anglos, Hispanics, Chinese, Arabs—it was frustrating to keep straight who was who. He found it so annoying that little flames popped up the sleeves of his long-sleeve dress shirt. He wore a British Turnbull and Assar stripped blue-and-white shirt, a light blue tie with embroidered fleur-de-lys, gray slacks from Harrods in London, and black boots from Carnaby Street. Everything had been ordered online and fetched by his demon network. The items were all particularly expensive as he had required them to be tailored with asbestos thread.

"Every one of you revert to your angel state," he commanded. "I want to see who the Hell is here."

Instantly the demons took on their heavenly forms. They were blond, handsome, and wore white robes. Satan looked face to face. Their heavenly names had been long forgotten by ancient humanity and replaced with the names given to them by the pagan peoples of the world. There was Brono and Fenrir from the Nordic clime. Baal-Hammon, Resheph, and Melqart from Mesopotamia. Hou-chi and Lu-hsing of China, and Fukurokuju from Japan. Zeus, Dionysus, and Hephaestus from Greece, and rounding out the group was Lono and Pele from Hawaii. They were majestic and manipulative gods. None of them had ever met a businessman they couldn't master. Lucifer loved them all.

"That's better, boys," he said. "Feels like only yesterday that you were poor, menial servants of Jehovah. Now you're the richest demi-gods in the universe. Well done."

All of the angels laughed and clapped enthusiastically. The Devil grinned happily and looked at them all.

"I haven't heard any rumors that you've misused your wealth beginning new charities or supporting legitimate governments. That makes me glad. I have to admit though—" and suddenly flames danced on Lucifer's arms and the top of his head, "—that I am furious that one of you masterminded the Trump presidency to create the wild ass tariffs that chief executive ordered, and you did it *without consulting me.*"

Satan stood up and bellowed.

"Which one of you was it?!" he shouted.

The angels literally cowered before Lucifer's titanic rage. Then he turned into a ball of fire spewing flames across the seated angels. They patted out the sparks that landed on their robes and hair and glowered at each other as if to say, "Are you the one? Admit it, you sumbitch!"

The fireball vanished and the Devil reappeared sitting in his chair. He looked relaxed and pleased.

"Good," he said. "None of you helped Trump. It appears that the moron managed to do it all by himself. Your job now is to make some money off those insane tariffs. Use your contacts to clog up the official channels and rake those custom taxes into my coffers."

Every angel nodded. None of them spoke.

"I also need your help in finding out who has declared a holy war on the SEALs down here. Not only have several of Hell's citizens been murdered, the bastards are carrying the fight into the streets of New Babylon. I will not tolerate that. I want the jihadists identified wherever they are on Earth." He looked straight at Baal-Hammon, Resheph, and Melqart who controlled much of the commerce and politics in the Levant.

"My wife is sure that a terrorist cell is located somewhere in Saudi Arabia and is funded and protected by the Saudi royal family itself. Use your influence, your connections, and your money to find out who they are and where they are." Once again small tongues of flame appeared on Lucifer's shoulders and shirt sleeves. He raised his voice.

"This conflict is escalating and I will not have that! My own American contacts would like to send thousands of anti-terrorist troops to battle in my capital city. **I will not have that!** I want this finished. Now go. And don't let me down."

The Shapeshifter demons left without a word, each one bowing deeply to the Devil as they passed. Michael Rockefeller came into the boss's office. He found Satan carefully inspecting his shirt and slacks for burn marks.

"How did the meeting go, sir?" Michael asked.

Lucifer responded without looking up from his task.

"I think my greedy minions are prepared to go all-out to find who is funding our plague of assassins. Also, I tried out a pretend temper tantrum and flamed into a fireball." The Devil looked up at Michael and smiled. "These clothes did great!"

* * *

The SEALs in Hell initiated a large-scale sharing of ideas, thoughts, and plans to survive using several existing SEAL sites on Hell's internet. Within twenty-four hours of the last encounter between SEALs and Arabs, every SEAL had teamed up with a colleague. Thousands of rounds of various kinds of assault ammunition had been imported from Earth, and two teams numbering ten SEALs each had been formed to begin working their way through New Babylon seeking assassins. The sweep would include searching every building and every room in the capital city. Foc's'le Follies. Just without the ship.

No one worried about the risk or the danger. It was what they had done as SEALs when they were still alive on Earth. It was now what they'd do as SEALs damned to Hell. Each squad carried emergency mobile phones. If a call came from SEALs under attack they would respond and bullets would fly. Blood would be shed and lives lost. Little did they know how much blood and how many lives.

No sooner had A Team and B Team begun evening sweeps in opposite parts of New Babylon, both squads received emergency calls for back-up. Two SEALs in a small home near the city's northern edge were facing a squad of assassins. They had seen the attackers approaching and several of them had been immediately shot. The remainder took cover behind trees and fences and returned fire.

The besieged sailors left the back of the home and crawled on their bellies around the house. They reached the front yard where the assassins were concealed. One of them suddenly stood up and put a thick, short rifle-like weapon to his shoulder. Both SEALs recognized it as an American manufactured XM-25 grenade launcher. They fired their automatic rifles at the man. The Kalasnaikov Concern in the hands of one SEAL and the Remington Arms Bushmaster in the hands of the other drove a sustained burst of bullets into the enemy's body, but not before he fired his grenade.

The grenade shot into the house and its resulting explosion tore off the roof, blew out everything in the home, and set fire to the structure. Assassins surrounded their dead colleague and fired in the direction where the shots that killed him had originated. Both SEALs had crawled into a neighbor's yard, then stood behind a steel storage shed and fired at the attackers. Within two minutes a SEAL team arrived and surrounded the Arab shooters. Then the real firefight began. Hundreds of rounds of automatic fire were exchanged.

The other SEAL team arrived and attacked the enemy's rear with automatic rifles blazing. Several of the assassins fell as they charged the SEALs firing behind them. Three sailors were killed and the remaining Arab shooters fled into the neighborhood beyond. Residences were dark with doors locked as terrified families hoped that whatever terrible conflict was happening outside would not spill into their homes.

Word got to Lucifer almost instantly and he ordered a hundred Samn demons to join the search for the assassins. As the wave of demons began to crisscross the neighborhood, the assassins simply disappeared. Gunfire was silenced and both the SEALs and the Samns checked houses, garages, and sheds, searching for the retreating assassins. After forty-five minutes of searching, the SEALs stopped.

Mili and Mardie arrived at the scene and studied the casualties. Young Arab terrorists and white-haired American SEALs lay sprawled out across the impromptu battlefield. Mili talked to the special forces personnel who had survived.

There was no trace of where the killers had gone. Vanished was probably a better word. The mystery lasted only as long as it took Lucifer to join them. He searched the area where the shooters had been last seen. He pointed towards a spot near a tall picket fence.

"There's a wormhole right there." Jehovah and angels could see wormholes. They could also be found by scientific types using algorithms generated by supercomputers like IBM's Watson. Or by geniuses like Albert Einstein who was the first mathematician to theorize the existence of wormholes, and Hugh Grant III, the physicist whose Many Worlds theory purposed them as travel passages.

Lucifer conferred with the SEAL squad leaders and explained that the assassins had used the wormhole to escape. In fact, they had very likely used that same hole to enter Hell. How had they found it? Were traitorous demons helping the killers? And more pressing at this point, was the question: where had they gone?

Both A Team and B Team volunteered to enter the wormhole and find out. The Devil asked B Team to take on the mission. It had sustained the least casualties. He told them to double-up on weapons, ammunition, and water. He also told them to scribble out any last words they wished to leave behind. Wherever they traveled to find the men who had murdered their comrade, there was no guarantee they would return.

Every SEAL on the team stood fast on their desire to go in hot pursuit of the assassins. Each man was dressed in camouflaged khaki fatigues, heavy black boots, and a helmet. There was some joking and laughing as they prepared to enter the hole. Perhaps it was to break the tension or ease the fear of the unknown. Lucifer, Mili, and Mardie stood watching. And even they laughed when a tall, muscular, curly-haired SEAL cracked, "I'm coming back," he said. "I survived three marriages."

He gave everyone a thumbs up. Hours later when he was one of only two SEALs who returned from their mission, he gave the same thumbs up. Good thing there hadn't been any of his ex-wives among those shooting on the other side.

CHAPTER SEVEN

The two SEALs who returned from the wormhole raid sat in Lucifer's office. Lieutenant Bill Iverson, who had now survived three marriages *and* wormhole travel, sat with Captain Bob Tanke who had led the mission. The captain was fit and buff, a handsome man with a crewcut. Lucifer had introduced Mili and Mardie who were present and then asked Tanke to share what had happened after his squad of ten men had entered the wormhole into other space.

"We grouped for rollcall," Tanke began, "after stepping out into a wilderness desert area. The terrain was dry and the only vegetation was a shrub that resembled sage brush, dry and bushy. There was no one in sight, but we were able to pick up the assassins' tracks in the sand. There appeared to be four terrorists ahead of us. We spread out to avoid presenting a single target and I followed the tracks keeping a slight lead on the squad.

"A scab rock escarpment appeared in the distance. Maybe sixty feet high, it was as flat and as long as a football field. A plateau rising in the desert. I beckoned to Iverson and we went ahead. A helicopter dropped out of the sky and flew directly at us.

"The chopper was a UH-60M Blackhawk, a US attack helicopter. There were no identification markings of any kind. It fired two rockets at the squad behind us and blew them into the air like ragdolls. One downed SEAL managed to fire his weapon at the belly of the chopper as it swept over to view the massacre. The big bird exploded mid-air, flinging machine fragments almost as far as where Iverson and I were standing two hundred yards away.

"As the helicopter went down enemy fire erupted from atop the butte at the SEAL who'd taken the helicopter down. He was returning fire from his own weapon while Iverson and I circled behind the rocky height and climbed its backside. We spotted the four Arabs shooting at our remaining teammate. They stood less than a hundred yards away. Iverson and I took them out like ducks at a carney show.

"We scrambled back down the butte and ran to the SEAL who'd been engaging the snipers. He lay with a massive hole in his back where they had shot him despite his prone position on the desert ground. This SEAL, who'd done his last heroic deed, was Jon Symonds, a good man from Seattle who'd kept the shooters busy until we could finish them. The rest of our men had been killed in the helicopter attack. We took their rifles to memorialize them, returned to the wormhole, and stepped back into Hell."

Mili had a question.

"Captain, was it your impression that the four Arabs you and Iverson shot on the rocky butte were the same assassins who escaped from Hell through the wormhole?"

"Yes, ma'am," he answered. "They were dressed in identical black jeans and black

T-shirts and were clearly the same shooters we chased through the New Babylon neighborhood." Tanke frowned slightly. "I was surprised that we had stepped out of the wormhole into empty wilderness. I had expected to find a support base or some kind of military facility. Instead, there was nothing. I still think there has to be a base nearby.

It should be located and destroyed as it is where the enemy deploys its assassins to enter Hell."

"I agree, Captain," Lucifer responded. "Thank you for doing your job." Satan looked at Lieutenant Iverson. "And thank you, Lieutenant. I am glad that you and your commanding officer are back safely." Both Tanke and Iverson rose and left Lucifer's office. The Devil picked up his secure office landline phone and spoke to a senior Samn demon in the field. He ordered the wormhole to be guarded around the clock, and any person using it to enter Hell was to be shot without question. Satan hung up.

"Your thoughts?" he asked his wife. Mili and Mardie got up from their chairs and stood next to the Devil's desk.

Mili spoke up.

"I would like to know what country lies on the other side of the wormhole. I would also like to know the ownership of the unmarked helicopter that attacked the SEALs. That is a very expensive and a very hard to obtain piece of American military hardware. Terrorists didn't acquire it, but their sponsors were obviously able to."

Lucifer nodded.

"The price tag for the chopper is six million dollars and change. One also has to wonder how many more of them the assassins may possess."

Mardie raised another worrying point.

"I am also concerned about the existence of other holes that will allow more Arab gunmen to enter Hell."

Satan nodded.

"I am, too," he agreed.

"The logistics of this whole nightmare are beginning to spin out of control," Mili said, obviously despairing about the desperate situation developing in Hell.

Satan shook his head.

"No. It's a simple numbers game. Who has the most soldiers. Who has the most guns. Who has the most determination. I will post Samns throughout the city with orders to engage anyone entering or exiting Hell via any wormhole. Further, I am going to ask Captain Tanke to reform B Team and reenter the space hole we know about.

"I want to know what country is sending assassins into Hell. I want to know what facilities and how many shooters are located near that hole. I am inclined to think that a lot of time and preparation has been invested in the enemy's plan, and I am going to find out by whom and why. It's not really just a detective's game anymore. It has escalated into a war. However, the pieces of this puzzle are starting to fall into place. I need you and Mardie to assemble them for me so I can end this threat once and for all."

Lucifer walked over to Mili and reached for her hand.

"I need you more than ever, Mili. What will it take to strengthen your resolve?"

Mardie answered for her sister.

"If it were me, I'd offer her cake balls."

Mili laughed hard and so did Lucifer. Fact was though, the promise of a time of peace celebrated with chocolate-dipped cake balls was the hope of normalcy that sealed the deal.

✳ ✳ ✳

A man bearing an automatic Polish FB Radom rifle walked silently through the orchards next to the Ben-Yehuda Kibbutz. He entered the settlement where the public buildings and dormitories were located. His name was David Al-Din.

He had been an Arab Christian in Bethlehem, killed during an Israeli military response to a protesting Palestinian crowd that had gathered in the town's main square. Why the Jews had so forcefully intervened he did not know, but he had picked up a rifle dropped by a fallen soldier and shot two IDF soldiers with it before being shot himself.

Now New Babylon was filled with street fighting. American soldiers were battling Arab gunmen. It struck David that it was time for him to avenge himself on the Jews hidden by the storm of violence that had enveloped Hell. He had long ago purchased a smuggled Radom assault rifle. It was used and old, but he had been able to afford it and had kept the weapon hidden for the day when it would be useful once again. He was carrying it now.

It was mid-morning when he crossed the parking lot in front of the kibbutz library. He recognized it from images on the internet. He also knew which building housed the high school. It was behind the library on the right. No one was outside. He walked up to the doors of the high school and pulled one open. A slight echo of conscience touched him as he walked in. These were just young people. They had been born down here and were not responsible for the sins of their people. Yet he was sure that they were being raised to despise Arabs and kill them without conscience.

Resolved to do what he came to do, David walked down the silent hallway to the first classroom. He looked in through the small window in the door. The room was full of young students at their desks facing a teacher at the front of the room, a woman who was not so much older than her students. She instinctively spun her head to the right and looked at him. He turned the doorknob and went in.

✳ ✳ ✳

Mili and Mardie arrived at the kibbutz. Pfot had driven them out immediately after word had reached Lucifer that a lone gunman with an assault rifle had entered a kibbutz classroom and shot the teacher and as many students as he could before his ammunition ran out. He fled from the classroom having been inside no more than sixty seconds. Seventeen teenagers were dead. Another six had been wounded but would survive. They were being watched and guarded in the kibbutz infirmary.

David Ben-Gurion had personally called Mili on her mobile. She was at home doing wash while Sriracha and Jesus were sleeping in. Lucifer had gone into the field with his contingent of Samns searching for additional wormholes used by the Arab terrorists, and to prep Captain Tanke for B Team's re-entry into the already identified hole.

Mili saw David's ID on the monitor and answered.

"Hello, David."

"Dear Mili," he said. "Please sit down."

"Oh, God," Mili moaned. "Is it Little Mardie?"

"Please sit. I have news that will break your heart."

Mili sat. Her hands shook as she held her mobile phone to her ear. David waited and then spoke quietly, with great heaviness in his voice.

"Little Mardie has been shot," he said and stopped. Mili cried out in anguish.

"How?" she asked.

"A man with an assault rifle entered her classroom here at the kibbutz. Seventeen high school students were killed. Little Mardie was one of them. Arie died as well. I am so sorry."

Mili sat in shock. It couldn't be true. Little Mardie was not dead. It was a mistake. She could not be dead. It was impossible.

"Are you sure, David?" she asked.

"Yes, Mili. We have set up a temporary area in the library for the victims' bodies. Mardie has been moved there. She has been tended and washed and only needs you to be at her side." Ben-Gurion paused. He couldn't speak. His emotions overcame the old warrior. Never, never, never could he stay strong when children died.

"Come as soon as you can, Mili," he finally said, sobbing.

"Thank you, David. Thank you for calling me. I could not have heard this from anyone else but you."

Mili pushed the *Off* button and slipped from her kitchen chair onto the tiled floor. She wept and keened with her hand over her mouth so as to not wake Sriracha and Jesus. Her daughter was dead. Taken from her. Her times with Little Mardie flashed through her mind. Watching her gossip with Alice Roosevelt. Growing bored and cranky having to sit through Lucifer's bowling tournaments. Eating Ben and Jerry's ice cream at San Francisco's Fisherman's Wharf. Her first period. Her first pimple. Her first and only boyfriend, Arie Millatiner. The man she wanted to farm with. Have babies with. Grow old with. And now it was all vapor. Dreams that had died with Little Mardie and Arie, murdered in a school classroom, for God's sake.

Her sister called, weeping. She told Mili she'd heard about Little Mardie and Pfotenhauer was bringing her over. Mili told her they would all go to the kibbutz together and ended the call.

She got up off the floor and washed her face. But she kept on crying, knowing that her tears for her dead daughter would never end.

Mardie arrived and let herself into the house. She put her arms around her twin and held her while they both wept. Mili could hardly function. Mardie helped her get dressed in black slacks and a gray blouse, and she held her hand as they went out to the car. Pfotenhauer had waited next to the car. He was weeping and could barely murmur his condolences to Mili. She hugged him and then got into the back seat of the Tesla. Mardie hugged Pfotenhauer as well. He closed her door after she entered the back seat next to Mili.

"Are you all right to drive?" Mardie asked Pfot after he was in the driver's seat. He nodded.

"I can do it for Little Mardie," he said, and cried gently as he pulled the car onto the street.

The trip to the kibbutz was silent except for a brief call from Lucifer who told Mili that he would be joining her at the kibbutz. He was calm and serious. Every single day of Little Mardie's human life, he knew that someday she would be taken away. He accepted it. He planned for it. And though the shock of her murder was breaking his heart, he had things to talk to his wife about.

David Ben-Gurion came out of the library, the makeshift place of the dead. The young people who had died were laid on tables covered with sheets. Many parents were inside, and two Israeli men controlled how many grieving adults entered the room of the dead children.

David embraced Mili and Mardie together and held them tight for a long moment. He had cried his tears for the slain students and his eyes were red and swollen. He had no words for his friends the Wickett sisters. He simply stood quietly, holding their hands while they wept. Tears streamed down their cheeks and dropped to the ground. Moshe Dayan appeared and hugged the women. He, too, did not speak. What God hath wrought he had learned long ago just to accept. *If* there was a God. He didn't know. What he did know was that the kibbutz had been plunged into grief and that no one would ever be the same again.

One of the men watching the doors to the library came and told Mili that she and Mardie could enter. Mili was supported by Mardie's arm around her waist and walked up the steps to the library. Inside she gave her name to a woman who nodded sadly, and then led her to the table where Little Mardie lay with a sheet pulled up to her shoulders.

Mili looked down at her daughter. Little Mardie's face was drawn, but peaceful. Her blonde hair was combed back and her eyes were closed. Dear God, Mili thought. It was her Little Mardie and she was truly gone. She curled her fingers and touched her daughter's cheek with the back of her hand.

Her skin was cool, but not cold. Yet it would never warm to life again. Her lungs would not rise. Her heart would not beat. Her eyes would not open. Never again would her laugh echo at mealtime. Never again would her admonitions make her brother Sriracha grin. Never again would she tease Jesus about eating his vegetarian meat. Never again would Mili hear her say, Mom, I love you so much. It was all gone. Every aspect of her life with her eldest child and only daughter was forfeit and lost. Oh, God, how could this have happened?

Mili put her hands to her face and moaned. Tears flooded her eyes again and Mardie led her out of the room and back outside. Mili sat down in a chair next to David Ben-Gurion and Mardie stood crying next to her. Then a firm hand tenderly held Mili's shoulder. She opened her eyes to see that Lucifer was standing before her. She leaned forward into his body and cried all the more. He held her in his strong arms and gently rocked his grieving wife. After a long time, he knelt in front of Mili and looked into her eyes.

"Little Mardie is not here, my love," he said gently. "But she is not gone. I am leaving to talk to Jehovah. I swear to you that you will see her again, alive and smiling."

Mili looked into her husband's tender eyes and realized that he was right. She reached for his hands and squeezed them hard. Little Mardie had died a human life after which God himself reserved the right to judge her eternity.

"Go now, love," she urged. "Go now!"

CHAPTER EIGHT

Lucifer stepped out into Heaven in full view of God's temple. He crossed the great outer courtyard and stood in front of the golden doors of Jehovah's home. The Archangel Michael was there. He was sitting on a chair and had a Mac portable on his lap. He closed the lid and watched the Devil approach.

He stood up and set his laptop on his chair. He was wearing a white robe and his hair was pulled into a pony tail down his back. Lucifer wore a silver robe and a golden crown signifying his role as ruler of Hell. God liked it when the boys dressed up a bit. He always wore a robe himself and enjoyed both its look and feel.

"Hello, Lucifer," Michael said as his fellow Archangel approached.

"Hello, Michael," Satan said and extended his hand and shook Michael's.

"Word has reached us of your tragedy," Michael said. His face looked serious and concerned. "How are you and your wife?"

Lucifer was surprised at Michael's acknowledgement of his grief. His fellow Archangel had only celebrated death before. Now he seemed to share in mourning it.

"It is unlike any sorrow we have ever experienced, brother," the Devil told him. "The complete and utter loss of our daughter under such terrible circumstances brought grief beyond description." Satan paused and looked at Michael. He was sharing his pain and it frankly astonished him. "Thank you for your sympathy."

Michael nodded.

"You are here to see Jehovah?"

Lucifer nodded.

"He is expecting you."

Satan watched as Michael opened a huge door for him.

"Follow me," Michael told him. "He is concerned for you and only wants to help."

Jehovah only wants to help, the Devil thought? He was not used to that and it made him suspicious. Since when had the Almighty wanted to help anybody? He walked in after Michael and headed for God's living room.

✳ ✳ ✳

Mili sat at her kibbutz kitchen table with both David and Paula Ben-Gurion. David wore black slacks and a long-sleeve white dress shirt. His wife wore a long black dress with a high neck and long sleeves. Paula had made coffee for everyone and served streusel cake that she had brought. Unsaid was that the living had to go on living. Everyone drank coffee and ate the cake.

Pfotenhauer had taken Mardie back to Mili's house in New Babylon. She would keep an eye on Sriracha and Jesus until Mili and Lucifer came to break the awful news about Little Mardie and Arie.

Mili's demeanor was still grief-stricken. But certain things had to be addressed. David was gentle but covered the hard issues in front of Mili.

"Most of the young people who were killed will be buried according to the Jewish tradition that requires burial within twenty-four hours of death. The burials will take place at dusk and we will hold a memorial service for the victims." Mili looked at Ben-Gurion and listened carefully. "Little Mardie converted to Judaism," David went on. "Therefore, I need to ask you if you wish to have her buried tonight as well. You must decide now, and it may cause Lucifer and your other children to miss saying goodbye."

Mili nodded. She had no idea how to answer. She had to make decisions by herself. Did she want her sons to view their dead sister's body? She had no idea when Lucifer planned to return from Heaven. Would he be hurt and angry if Little Mardie were already buried when he returned? She had to have more time to think.

She turned to a different subject. One that was becoming a growing obsession for her.

"Did anyone see the shooter?"

Ben-Gurion shook his head.

"He fled the classroom before anyone got a good look at him. He disappeared into the citrus groves."

"He acted on his own?"

"Apparently," David answered. "Moshe believes that he took advantage of the chaotic conditions in Hell right now, with the Arab assassins infiltrating and the SEALs trying to protect themselves. A solo assassin with some grudge to avenge entered the fragile heart of the kibbutz and killed our children." Ben-Gurion teared up and Paula reached for his hand.

Mili continued.

"Were the bullet casings saved?" she asked.

"Of course," David replied. "We had them couriered to Lucifer's headquarters to be examined in his forensics lab. The killer used an assault rifle, so theoretically whoever sold it to him may be able to identify the buyer."

That was optimistic, Mili thought. Satan had managed to reduce the number of demons in the gun trade, but more guns than ever seemed to be entering Hell. Finding the dealer who had sold the murderer his rifle would be hard, and getting him to admit it would be even harder. With the Devil's own daughter among the victims, the guilty smuggler might well choose to flee to avoid being found out.

"What time will the service be?" she asked David.

"Around nine o'clock this evening," he answered. "Just as the sun sets."

Mili had only the afternoon to talk to Mardie and try to get a message to Lucifer. Time would pass quickly while she addressed these issues. But remembering as she would, over and over, that Little Mardie was dead, would make it seem like a lifetime.

✳ ✳ ✳

Michael walked down the entry hall inside the temple. Lucifer followed him. The passage was open and empty, its steep vertical marble walls hung with golden shields. Looking up, Satan saw the peaked roof. Massive cedar beams met at the apex where a seam of stained glass let the light in. Michael entered the antechamber at the end. The Holy of Holies. The Devil followed.

The room was decorated with ancient bronze lamps, filled with olive oil and lit by cotton wicks placed in holes in the tips. There was a giant television screen—large enough to virtually cover one wall—as big as most theater movie screens. There was a large, cushioned recliner with pillows where Jehovah sat watching the two Archangels enter.

He was barefoot wearing a long white robe covering his shoulders and arms and falling down to the middle of his calves. Long wavy black hair flowed over his shoulders. His face was quite handsome. He looked like a young George Clooney. Had God been watching the old Oceans movies? Both Michael and Lucifer knew that Jehovah tended to look like whichever actor he had just viewed. They'd seen him as debonair Clark Gable, honest Jimmy Stewart, brilliant Benedict Cumberbatch, and even self-deprecating and charming Robert Downey, Jr.

However, the Lord never looked like a famous politician. Nor a famous television evangelist. Not too hard to figure out that he watched neither the news nor the megachurch cheerleading services. Satan had wondered somewhat disrespectfully at times if Jehovah was jealous of the acclaim and wealth of the evangelical television superstars. He knew, but had never revealed to God, that Pastor Joel Osteen's net worth was considerably more than Jehovah's.

"WELCOME MICHAEL SACRED SHIELD AND LUCIFER MORNINGSTAR,"

God declared loudly. His voice would have shattered mortal eardrums. It only buzzed a bit inside the Archangels' ears. Didn't make it any more pleasant, however.

"Just kidding, fellas," the Almighty declared, laughing at his own pomposity.

The Lord used a normal speaking voice to welcome Michael and Lucifer. He sounded like he was in a good mood. Always a bonus, Satan thought, when there was negotiating to be done. He did not think of Little Mardie as being dead. Just absent. If he had his way, he'd fix that today.

God watched Lucifer as though waiting for him to speak his mind. The Devil knew that Jehovah was aware of his personal loss. As he was aware of every human death. Yet in all the eons he had watched Jehovah and talked to him about people passing and being judged, Jehovah had never expressed sadness, nor regret, nor any kind of emotional empathy for the deceased or their loved ones. He would have nothing to say now about the tragedy and Lucifer's loss.

While the Devil had not seen it firsthand, Gabriel had been with Jehovah when Jesus had been nailed to a Roman cross. God did not speak of it. Afterwards, he never acknowledged that his son was crucified, dead, and buried. Why should Lucifer be surprised at all that God had nothing to say about Little Mardie's death?

"Lord," the Devil began. "There was an incident in Hell today where a man with a military assault rifle murdered a group of young people." Satan was careful not to mention the kibbutz or the high school. He did not have any idea whether Jehovah was aware of those places in Hell. As far as God knew, it was all brimstone and fire for the damned.

"I am aware that many young adults were slain today," Jehovah responded. "Are you here to request replacements for their Hellion bodies?"

"These young people were actually the human children of families in Hell."

Jehovah frowned.

"*Human* offspring of Hellion parents?"

"Yes."

"How is that even possible?" God demanded to know.

"I can't explain it, Lord. But many Hellions have sired children. My wife, Mili, and I have three children. And today one of them was killed in the massacre."

"Mardell Morningstar," God replied. "Your daughter. Yes. I know. She and her decent and kind boyfriend are staying with me in Paradise. They are deserving, wonderful kids. I hope you will be happy for them."

"All things considered, Lord of the Universe, Mili and I were hoping that you would allow Little Mardie and Arie to return to Hell."

"Egad, Lucifer!" God bellowed. **"Are you out of your mind? Back to fire and ash? Starvation and want?"** Jehovah stopped speaking, then resumed in a normal voice. "They can be together up here. Forever happy. Gone from that place of sorrow, tears, and suffering."

Satan stared at Jehovah. The deity really didn't know what was going on in Hell. It was experiencing an American-style post-World War II boom. Repaired infrastructure, plentiful food, untainted water, full employment—and just like America—a whole batch of national parks with mountains, forests, lakes, *and* camping sites. The sun shone. The sky was cloudless. And everyone's happy mood was due to their belief that Hell was now every bit as nice as California.

"Mili and I will miss her, Lord. She is not even twenty-one."

"It doesn't matter how old she is," Jehovah replied placatingly. "Her worries are over. Her anxieties and fears are gone. Why would you ever want to make her return to life in Hell?"

How could Lucifer explain that life in Hell was vibrant, and challenging, and worrisome, but that those were the very things that enriched human existence. Heaven—when he had lived here ages ago—had been excruciatingly boring. As it had been for the first humans in the Garden of Eden, too. Was it an accident that Adam and Eve sinned to break free of a meaningless life of lethargy and boredom? When God kicked them out of the Garden of Eden and warned Adam that he was now condemned to work by the sweat of his brow to feed himself and Eve, the poor bastard probably felt like cheering.

"In Hell," Satan tried to explain, "Little Mardie was hoping to farm with Arie, to raise a family, and to live out a complete life cycle with aging and death after a full life. She has been robbed of all those things, Lord. I would like her to still have them."

Jehovah regarded Lucifer with a churlish expression.

"Your child is free from all the disadvantages and problems in Hell. Surely you must know that I am aware of the street fighting spreading throughout your capital city. What happens when it spreads to other cities and villages? How will you be able to protect Mardie and Arie then? You're going to have your hands full just keeping Mili and your boys alive."

The Devil flushed with anger and embarrassment.

"Will you at least consider my request?" he dared to ask.

"No."

Lucifer stared at Jehovah. The self-declared I AM WHO I AM. The mercurial God who proudly boasted I WILL BE WHO I WILL BE. Asshole.

✳ ✳ ✳

Satan stayed for a long time anyway arguing with the Almighty about Little Mardie's future. Jehovah was not ornery and did not kick Satan out. But he was divinely convinced that Mardie and Arie, and, in fact, *all* of the young folks who had been murdered were in fact going to be saints and live up here in Heaven. God found it fascinating that Lucifer continued to champion family life in Hell over Heaven's bliss.

Perhaps his newly restored Archangel had forgotten the endless comforts of salvation. Heaven was not without occasional issues and problems. Gabriel's death by a gunshot wound was witness to that. But that was a rare discomfort, an unlikely event, as opposed to every SEAL in Hell having to watch out for his buddies and sleep with his Bushmaster, AEK-971, or Uzi at night. He listened to the Devil's arguments, but he did not change his mind. Because he was right.

"Lu, I am persuaded that Little Mardie will be happy up here." God's expression was benign and his eyes almost sympathetic. "You may come and see her whenever you wish. You and Mili and your boys and your sister-in-law."

Lucifer thanked God and bowed his head. It was not what he and Mili wanted. But it was what he and his wife would accept.

Satan lifted his head and met Jehovah's gaze. He had one last request.

"May I see her now?"

God nodded, and then smiled.

"She is waiting for you."

Mili's sister Mardie had stayed with Sriracha and Jesus. She fixed them macaroni and cheese for dinner then watched a movie on the telly by herself, wiping away any stray tears with her handkerchief. Sriracha played video games and Jesus worked on his Hebrew vocables. He had learned to speak the language fluently, but he wanted to write it as well.

His goal after that was to learn Koine Greek so he could read the New Testament in its original language. Mardie had no idea what he was going to do with all that religious learning. Be a priest?

Mili attended the interment of the young people. David and Paula stood on either side of her with their arms around Mili's waist. Each victim's body had been wrapped in a white shroud and lowered into individual graves. Mili dropped a handful of soil onto Little Mardie's body. She had not gone back into the library to look at her a second time. Once had been enough to dislodge every living image of her daughter. In time that might change, but her true hope was to see her alive again after she had entered into eternal life.

Weeping parents and thousands of members of the kibbutz stood together in the settlement's parking lot while David Ben-Gurion led the memorial service. It was secular. There were no prayers or hymns. The traditional Jewish Kaddish commending the dead to the God of life and death was not sung. These Jews had no regard for that God. Neither did Mili. When David recited the names of the murdered students and the names of their parents everyone wept. This moment was the truest and most profound memorial to the beloved children who were gone.

Mili went to bed alone. More alone than she had ever felt in her life. She wept. She tossed and turned. She slept in fits and starts. In the middle of the night Lucifer came to bed and held her tight. It took a long while, but Mili finally fell asleep. Ending the worst day of her life. There was nothing more to think or say.

CHAPTER NINE

In the morning, Lucifer and Mili returned to their home in New Babylon. Pfotenhauer drove them, and then left to be alone by himself. Little Mardie's death weighed on his old heart, and nothing but time would lift that burden.

Lucifer told Mili that he had seen Mardie in Heaven.

"She was standing with Arie. She misses you. But she is all right, love. Mardie looked radiant. She was beautiful and happy, and looked like an angel. Arie was holding her hand and smiling. They both hugged me and said they would miss being in Hell, especially the work and satisfaction that everyone shared in the kibbutz. Little Mardie asked that you come and visit as soon as you can."

Mili wished with all her heart that Little Mardie would have been allowed to return home, but she could live with seeing her up in Heaven. What was most important was that she was alive. And that she and Arie would still share an eternity together. A tear came to Mili's eye and she sat thinking her own thoughts for a while.

Lucifer silently reflected on a very emotional conversation he'd had early that morning with David Ben-Gurion. They'd walked in the orange groves and Ben-Gurion was ready to retaliate for the deaths of the kibbutz young people.

"Lucifer," he began, "as you likely know, every Israeli here served in the military. There is very strong sentiment that we be allowed to form a brigade to join the Navy SEALs and your demons in searching for the assassins who have turned Hell into a battle zone. We are confident that we would be of value as part of the operation to locate and destroy the terrorists."

The Devil stopped and faced Ben-Gurion.

"My dear friend," he said. "What that would do, I'm afraid, is turn Hell into another Middle East. Jews killing Arabs. Arabs killing Jews. What I have now is bad enough with two military groups pitting their skills against each other. But at least it's not two religions, two cultures, or two peoples tearing each other to pieces. The SEALs have a history of violence. They are facing a payback, but they will win and they will survive.

"You and the Israelis on the kibbutz have hammered your swords into plowshares as the Bible prophesied you would do. One lone wolf has penetrated your idyll and wrought havoc and destruction. But it is only one. We will find him and he will pay. I promise you. This is not the time to expand our fight into a war that might never end."

Satan put his hand on David's shoulder.

"You are a peacemaker now, old warrior. Give me a chance to do my job. Give Hell a chance to be the place where old vendettas and old wounds can heal. Our adversaries are not from down here. Let us not allow them to destroy what is ours."

"We only want to help," David said. He looked weary and frustrated. Seventeen children in his community had been slain. Was there a greater burden to carry as the leader of the kibbutz? Yet when he looked at Lucifer, he knew that there was. Satan's own daughter had been murdered. Ben-Gurion hung his head.

"David, you have important work to do," Lucifer told him. "The families who have lost their boys and girls need your attention and support. Take up that task and leave the defense of our beloved land in my hands."

Lucifer and Mili had decided not to tell Sriracha or Jesus about Little Mardie's death yet. He would take everyone to see her in Heaven and explain what had happened then. It felt like somewhat of a betrayal of the boys' right to know the truth, but it was what he and Mili thought best.

Mardie greeted Mili and Satan stoically, but the boys were happy and talkative. Lucifer went to his office to work with Captain Tanke on plans to lead his squad back through the assassins' wormhole. Mili asked Mardie to please stay for tea and to talk with her. Mardie agreed. She was willing to be whatever her grieving sister needed her to be.

"Have you eaten?" Mardie asked her sister when she served her tea and set down sugar and cream.

"I'm not hungry," Mili told her.

Without asking, Mardie opened a package of short bread cookies and filled a large plate. She put it on the kitchen table and then sat down with her own black tea. She watched Mili pick up a cookie and nibble at it absentmindedly.

"It was surreal, Mardie," Mili said quietly. "There was my Little Mardie wrapped up in a sheet, lying at the bottom of a dirt hole. Men from the kibbutz filled it. They filled all the holes while the parents watched the horror and wept. The bodies were buried in the corner of the orchard next to the kibbutz. Small pieces of cardboard with their names were stuck on metal rods by each grave. David Ben-Gurion told me that the site would be turned into a proper cemetery with each grave marked with a white-washed cement mastaba like they do in Israel. The names of every child will be noted on the memorials." Mili fell silent and ate her cookie. She reached for another one.

"I wish I could have been there with you," Mardie said softly.

Mili shook her head.

"You were with me for the awful part. Seeing Little Mardie lying on the table in the library. One can imagine a parent being dead. Or a friend. I found it easy to visualize myself as a corpse during my years at the Yard. But no one ever thinks about their child being dead. Laid out motionless. There and yet not there. Absent. Irretrievably gone.

"The only good news," Mili went on, "is that Little Mardie has already been welcomed to Heaven by Jehovah himself. He let Lu see her and while I wanted her down here with me, Lucifer said she was happy and so pleased that Arie was with her. Lucifer called his parents and shared the news. They were just glad that he was all right and not just the boy in the shroud lying in the hole in the graveyard."

"His parents didn't believe in Heaven?" Mardie asked.

"They did. But like most Jews down here they'd rather be at the kibbutz then dwell in Jehovah's Heaven."

"Well, Arie's with Little Mardie now," Mardie said.

Mili got up, opened her purse, which was sitting on a cupboard, reached in, and then sat back down at the table. She stretched her hand out toward Mardie and put an empty bullet cartridge on the table in front of her. Mardie picked it up. There was still a faint smell of smoke from when the gunpowder inside had caught on fire from the hammer impact causing its gases to expand and propel the embedded slug. She looked up at Mili and put the shell down.

"Where did you get this?"

"It's one of the shells from the gun used to slaughter the kibbutz children."

"Why do you have it?"

Mili drilled Mardie with her blue eyes.

"I am going to find the killer."

"How do you know that he's still alive? A lot of the Arabs who've entered Hell are in body bags lying in the morgue."

"He's alive," Mili answered. "He is not part of the wave of terrorists attacking the SEALs. My guess is that he is in Hell because of atrocities against the Jews and took advantage of the chaos in the streets to come to the kibbutz seeking vengeance."

"You think he's an Arab?" Mardie asked.

"I do," Mili replied. "When inhabitants saw or learned of the recent Arab attacks, I believe it encouraged a lone Arab nursing his grudge, who chose to blend in to the violence and act on his foul impulses."

"Why would an Arab be in Christian Hell?" Mardie asked.

"Because he is or *was* a Christian. He likely grew up as an Arab in Palestinian lands occupied by Israel, and some event turned him bitter. If he *is* down here, we can run checks on Hell's admission files on Arab Christians. We'll also get Lucifer's forensics folks to match this shell with the kind of assault weapon that fired it."

Mardie gazed at Mili for a long moment. Her sister realized she was staring at her and spoke curtly.

"*What*, Mardie?" Mili snapped. "Is there a problem?"

"I get the feeling that you are taking on this hunt by yourself."

"I am going to find out who murdered Little Mardie if that's what you're talking about."

"By yourself."

"I'd like you to help me if you are willing."

"And what happens when you identify the killer? You'll have Lucifer and his demons take him in?"

"Why don't we wait until we actually know who the killer is before we talk about how we deal with him?"

Mardie sensed that her sister was uncomfortable with her questions. There could only be one reason why.

"I think, Mili, that we should talk about it *now*," Mardie answered slowly. "Because I am not so sure that you intend to bring him in."

Mili broke eye contact and reached for another cookie. It was never a good idea for a professional law enforcement officer to entertain thoughts of personal revenge. It muddied judgment. It marred the investigation. And it led to breaking the law. This time Mili didn't care. She was going to find her daughter's murderer and kill him herself.

✳ ✳ ✳

Captain Bob Tanke led his squad of SEALs through the hole in space after sending a scout in ahead. The B Team was dressed in camouflage khakis, helmets, and combat boots.

The scout had returned saying there were no hostiles visible, not even on top of the rocky escarpment where snipers had positioned themselves before. It was also quiet today in Hell. No new assassins had apparently entered. Perhaps because Samns had guarded the one entry point the Arabs seemed to have found giving them passage into the underworld.

Bob Tanke and his men hiked across the barren landscape. It reminded him of eastern Washington where he had grown up. As a kid, the dry land had been irrigated and was the source of the greatest wheat harvests in the world. Now it was once again abandoned wilderness as the cost of raising wheat in the US had become prohibitive. The land was still family owned, but the landowners were now teachers, golf course maintenance workers, cook's helpers in the hospital, and janitors at schools.

Tanke's father and uncles had been rich wheat farmers. Then wheat farming failed. He had declined to get some Joe job after high school and joined the navy where he trained to be a special forces SEAL. He had never regretted joining the SEALs for a single moment. And he'd missed the missions terribly when he had retired. But now, by God—the God who surely loved America—Tanke was back in gear and looking for targets. Life was good.

He called a stop after an hour. Ahead was a cluster of metal buildings that very much looked like a temporary military installation.

The base looked quiet, but Tanke sent two scouts to check it out. They returned ten minutes later to report that it was unoccupied. The captain led his men onto the base and told everyone to look for anything that might give evidence as to what or who had run this operation.

After half an hour the team reassembled. Tanke's third-in-command, Petty Officer Second Class Augie Sackman, handed over a stack of Saudi Arabian money. Riyals.

"Where was this?" Tanke asked. He'd known Sackman since kindergarten, going every year with his parents to the Sackman's farm to slaughter pigs and make homemade sausage. Augie was heavy and looked like a potato. Always had. Early in life he had decided that he'd have better luck with guns than girls.

"It was inside a desk in an office with three other desks," Sackman answered. "Nothing else there. Don't know why anyone would keep money in a drawer."

Tanke shrugged.

"Stick it in your pocket," Tanke told him. "You can buy me a drink in Riyadh next time we're there."

Sackman chuckled.

"That'll be the day," he said and tucked the bills in his pants pocket.

Tanke wondered if they were in Saudi Arabia now, kicking around a nameless deployment point where the assassins had been sent through the space hole into Hell. Even if it was Saudi Arabia, it didn't mean that the royal government was sponsoring the terrorists. Or, for that matter, that it even knew about the operation.

As Tanke stood alone with his thoughts, one of his men interrupted him.

"Excuse me, sir," he said. "It appears that there is movement a click to the north."

He handed his pair of field binoculars to Tanke. The captain looked at a cloud of dust being stirred up in the distance.

"Tanks!" he cried out. "Double time to the nearest camp building! Now!"

Tanke started for the large metal building at a run. He turned his head to make sure his men were following. They were. As he ran, he could see a dozen tanks in the distance moving at full speed. He figured it wouldn't take more than five minutes for them to make it to the base.

Then he looked up and saw four F-15 fighter jets descending on his position. All of his men saw them and hit the ground. Tanke could see that the jets were not heading for the tanks. Struck with the realization of what was happening, Tanke only had time to cry out, "Oh, my God! The planes are protecting the tanks! They're heading for the wormhole!" before rockets from the jets destroyed the entire area around the base. No SEAL was left alive to tell the story.

✶ ✷ ✶

Lucifer was at his office when his mobile rang. The ID said A. Michael. He remembered that Jack the Ripper's real name had been A. McAllister. He'd never personally spoken to A. McAllister. He thought he might know who A. Michael was, however.

"Does the A stand for Archangel?" he said, answering the phone.

"It does, indeed," his peer answered. "Don't usually have any reason to call you but Jehovah picked up a prayer that he thought belonged to you. He wanted me to forward it."

The Devil was surprised. God was not particularly interested in prayers. That's why he had Archangels. That's why he'd given Satan deceased Gabriel's old job of responding to mortal petitions.

"Yes?" Lucifer asked.

"Before I share it," Michael responded, "let me remind you that you *missed* this prayer and Jehovah had to get it over to you. Sloppy. If I were you, I wouldn't let that happen again."

Michael was right. Plunged into dealing with Little Mardie's death and trying to protect Hell from the Arab killers had distracted him from his duties.

"Thanks, Mike. I'll take that advice."

Michael looked smug and nodded.

"So, what is so urgent?" Satan asked.

"God said to tell you that this prayer was uttered by one Captain Bob Tanke. He said you'd likely know who that was. Anyway, the captain cried—and I quote him exactly—'Oh, my God! The planes are protecting the tanks! They're heading for the wormhole!'"

CHAPTER TEN

Lucifer had left his office by the time Mili and Mardie arrived. No one knew where he had gone, but his aide Michael Rockefeller said he'd finished a phone call and then left without a word to anyone.

"Michael," Mili asked. "Are you authorized to assist me?"

"Ma'am, Lucifer has instructed me to help you in any way that you ask."

"Me, too?" Mardie asked.

"Yes," Michael answered. "Except I am not allowed to procure alcohol, cigarettes, and prescription drugs. Or to go on a date."

"What?" Mardie cried outraged.

"That's not actually *all* true," Michael retreated. "I could fetch prescriptions for personal use."

"What about the date thing?"

Michael blushed.

"Lucifer said you'd break my heart."

Mardie looked amazed. Then she looked pissed. She turned to Mili.

"Did you know about this?"

"No, I swear!" Mili insisted.

"Well, I'm going to be having a chat with your old man," Mardie said.

"Leave me out of it," Mili told her. Mardie looked frustrated but kept any more thoughts to herself. Mili reached in her purse and handed the empty rifle shell to Michael.

"Please take this to Lucifer's forensics lab. It was recovered from the massacre at the Ben-Yehuda Kibbutz High School. I want to know what type of automatic rifle fired it."

Michael nodded and took the cartridge.

"I also need one of your file clerks to help me search Hell's admission records."

"No problem," Michael told her. "Everything back to 1960 has now been stored electronically. Please come with me."

Mili and Mardie followed Rockefeller out of Lucifer's office through an antechamber filled with the desks of the Devil's personal assistants, then down a hall and into a small office that had a desk, file cabinets, and a young woman sitting in front of a computer monitor. She stood up when Michael entered the room.

She was a short Black female who loved the Lord. She had sung in a South Side Chicago gospel choir until she committed adultery with the director. When he dumped her, she shot him, and then herself. Her job experience with the Illinois Department of Motor Vehicles made her the ideal bureaucrat to manage and update Hell's admissions records.

"Sonja," Michael said. "These ladies are Mili Morningstar and Mardie Wickett, the master's wife and his sister-in-law." Sonja bowed her head respectfully. "They are investigating the shooting at the kibbutz and would like your help searching admissions data. I am taking evidence to forensics, so please get started. I'll be back before you're done."

Sonja nodded and sat down facing the computer monitor.

"What kind of CPU are you accessing?" Mardie asked her.

"A Cray XC-50," Sonja answered.

"How fast is that?" Mardie asked.

"One petaflop of peak performance in one cabinet."

"What does that mean?"

"It means this computer will design algorithms to perform your search and answer your inquiry virtually instantaneously."

"Well, that's impressive," Mili responded. "I have several questions. I'll give them to you one at a time."

"Waiting on you," Sonja told her.

"The first thing I need is a list of Arab males down here."

Sonja typed on her keyboard. The screen filled with Arab names.

"How many is that?" Mili asked.

"Five hundred and fifty-six."

"Not very many," Mili commented surprised.

"So most Christian Arabs go to Heaven?" Mardie asked.

"Want me to check?" Sonja asked.

"You can do that?" Mili responded surprised again.

"Yes. I can hack into Heaven's computers."

"Maybe later then," Mili replied. "For now, please sort the names you've ID'd by cause of death."

The screen fluttered and discrete lists of names appeared.

"How many died in actions against Israel's authorities?" Mili asked.

"Sixty-one."

"Of those, how many of them were able to handle an automatic weapon?"

"None."

Mili scowled.

"That can't be right."

Sonja refreshed the inquiry.

"None," she repeated.

"Maybe the killer learned how to shoot down here," Mardie suggested.

"Please save that last search response," Mili told Sonja. "And thank you for the help."

"PDQ," Sonja said and grinned. "Pretty damn quick."

Mili led Mardie out of the admissions office.

"If you're right that the murderer learned to shoot down here," she told her sister, "then we'll wait for the ID on the empty shell and decide which gun runner is most likely to have supplied the shooter. There aren't that many left since Lucifer's crackdown after the Mormon massacre. And those who do remain specialize in what they procure."

"New or used?" Mardie guessed.

"Nope," Mili replied. "Pricey or cheap."

The Wickett sisters waited for Michael in Lucifer's office. The Devil's old asbestos furniture had been replaced with gorgeous maple and mahogany pieces. Mardie sat on one of the wooden chairs in front of Satan's desk and Mili sat in the black leather executive chair that Lucifer used.

"Oh," Mardie said. "Aren't you the brave one?"

Mili grinned mischievously.

"He sleeps in my bed. I can sit in his chair."

"Ha!" Mardie snorted.

"Do you remember the first times we met Lucifer?" Mili asked. "Flames on his head. Flames on his sleeves. Fireball on his chair."

"What a jerk," Mardie said. "How did you ever tame his temper?"

"Seven years on another world, remember?"

"And he fell in love with you," Mardie responded.

"He did," Mili said and smiled. "And all these years later he has regular furniture here in the office. Though he buys asbestos clothing that he thinks I don't know about."

"Isn't that a bit like adult diapers?" Mardie asked.

Mili laughed out loud.

"I'll ask him that exact question and get back to you."

Mardie winked at her sister.

"You don't have to tell him that it was me who asked."

Michael walked back in the room and put the spent casing on Lucifer's desk in front of Mili.

"It was shot from an automatic Polish FB Radom rifle, manufactured in the 1980s. It is a fairly rare gun down here as it was of relatively poor quality made under the Soviets. I took the liberty of checking with the three gun ranges in New Babylon about who might have taken lessons shooting one. Turns out one range employee remembered a man who trained for several weeks on a Radom a year or so ago. He remembered his name as David Al-Din. I checked our files and he is a resident with a city address in a quiet lower-class neighborhood."

Mili got up and went back to Sonja's office. In moments, Sonja had pulled up Al-Din's entry file. It showed his picture—a young Arab man with a serious expression—and listed his birth place as Bethlehem, Israel.

Mili looked at Mardie.

"Bingo," she said. "I win."

✳ ✳ ✳

Lucifer walked through the wormhole and stepped into Saudi Arabia. At least it looked like Saudi Arabia. Might have been Utah though. Or Uzbekistan. Wherever it was, the bleak landscape was barren and unattractive. Calling it Saudi Arabia would do well enough.

Satan thought of Captain Tanke's last words. "Oh, my God! The planes are protecting the tanks! They're heading for the wormhole!" Odd, Satan thought, that Jehovah would trouble to send along that solitary prayer to him. Sorted from billions of cries for help, why had God deigned to snag it and deliver it to him? Perhaps because Little Mardie had been killed and Jehovah wanted to help him? Right. Countless people were slain every day and none ever had a single one of their prayers heard or answered.

Still, Lucifer *was* one of his Archangels. Maybe Jehovah had a small soft spot in his heart after all. A very, very small soft spot. Or he liked SEALs more than he liked Arabs. Now *that* was a possibility. Brown dust in great billowing clouds blew into the sky churned by the tanks Tanke had seen advancing toward Hell's wormhole. Satan spotted the lead tank. He recognized it as an M1 Abrams manufactured by the US manufacturer General Dynamics.

He'd himself indirectly helped Saudi Arabia buy hundreds of them by supplying false information to the American government that the Saudi's neighbor Yemen was arming itself to invade. What a laugh. The outdated and poorly led Yemeni army couldn't have invaded Sesame Street. His planted intelligence was taken as good cred, however, and $888 billion worth of General Dynamic tanks and Raytheon anti-tank rockets were sold to the Saudi royals.

When the fast-moving lead tank was a thousand yards from the wormhole, Lucifer raised his right arm and shot a lightning bolt the size and strength of the bolts that appear in thunderstorms. It was the equivalent of ten billion volts, enough energy to power a small town for an entire day. Or to blow a hole the size of a small town in front of the Saudi tank. Which it did.

Dirt filled the air, but when it began to settle, Lucifer could see that the tank driver had simply opted to circle the great hole and was still heading for the portal entrance into Hell. The driver swiveled his gun and began firing his machine gun at whatever mysterious weapon had fired the ray of pure energy at him.

Lucifer hit the ground to keep from being shredded by the hail of tank bullets. As much as he hated to take lives, the Devil didn't want anyone in Hell to have to face these tanks. He also fancied staying alive himself. He raised his hand and fired a bolt directly at the Abrams tank. It blew apart. Pieces of fiery hot metal and flaming chunks of burning human flesh flew at least a hundred yards.

To Satan's amazement the destruction of the brigade's alpha tank did not even slow the rest of the tanks. They came on full speed shooting machine guns and rockets in his direction. One by one Lucifer destroyed the Abrams tanks until the desert was brimming with hundreds of burning pieces of man-and-metal debris. He shook his head. What a waste. The tank crews were off to judgment—Muslim Heaven or Hell—but the tanks were lost. Lucifer had mixed feelings about Saudis, but he liked Abrams tanks.

He was suddenly distracted by a rush of supersonic noise in the skies above. A formation of F-15 fighter jets flew out of the horizon and dropped down with him in their sights. With a quick release of more lightning bolts, Satan blew up each of the attack planes. Who had sent tanks and planes to take on Hell itself?

Lucifer felt flushed and adrenalized. Like he'd drunk too much caffeine. But now he was coming down. He may have been victorious, but he was truly sick at heart that he had had to kill so many men. Sweet Jesus. He had destroyed a dozen tanks, a formation of jets, and at least fifty soldiers and pilots. He felt no pleasure in his deeds. Just disgust. With himself. What a waste of men and material. And he had no idea how much more of this insanity there was to come.

He got to his feet and walked through the field of destruction. The Devil scoured the area until he found the remains of Captain Tanke and his SEALs. They had been blown apart by jet rockets. Satan went body to body. No one had survived. But he noted with pleasure and appreciation that although Bob Tanke lay dead—a massive wound in his chest—he had departed with a contented smile on his face.

Lucifer re-entered Hell and ordered a dozen Samns to use the wormhole to bring back the remains of the fallen SEALs. He had a courtesy visit to make. With Jehovah. The Almighty had gone out of his way to warn him of the tank incursion. He didn't go out of his way for anybody for anything. What had God been thinking?

✳ ✳ ✳

"I just wanted to thank you, sir, for passing the prayer request on to me through Michael."

Jehovah nodded benevolently. Michael nodded, standing next to Lucifer. Today the Almighty was looking like Brad Pitt again. He was definitely dipping into the Oceans movie franchise.

"That one caught my ear," God said. "I get pleas every day from desperate men at war, which, of course, is always and everywhere. But that one caught my attention because it was uttered by a Navy SEAL. They remind me of me. Heroic, patriotic, unstoppable, and fond of violence. What's not to like?

"I checked on the petitioner and saw that he feared that Hell itself was about to be breeched by an attack force of Abrams tanks. What in the world, I thought? Was Saudi Arabia trying to invade Hell? I thought you needed to know."

"Thank you, Lord. I am in your debt."

"You are *forever* in my debt, Lucifer Morningstar." Jehovah spat out angrily. "You tried to kill me, remember? Now you're just *more* in my debt."

Lucifer bowed his head. He had said his thank you and now he could go. Maybe. He waited a moment, but Jehovah had finished being both nice and not nice. Bi-polar bastard.

CHAPTER ELEVEN

Mili sat quietly at her kitchen table. Some moments she was filled with longing for Little Mardie and could barely breathe. Other moments she was overcome with blinding hate for the animal who'd killed her daughter. Mardie was right. When David Al-Din's face was in her head she wanted to kill him any way possible.

She looked up. Sriracha was standing in the kitchen doorway.

"Hello, honey," she said tenderly. Sriracha was upset.

"I just got a call from Sasha Cohen at school," he said. "He told me everything that you *didn't* tell me. And he said he was sorry about Little Mardie."

Mili rose and put her arms around Sriracha. At fifteen he was almost as tall as her. He hugged her back, desperate and needy.

"I am so sorry," Mili told him. "I wanted to wait to tell you until I knew about Little Mardie. I know now."

Sriracha pulled back and looked in his mother's face.

"What do you mean?"

"Little Mardie is not here, but she is not gone," Mili said softly. "She and Arie are in Heaven. They are safe and they are together."

"How do you know that?"

"Your father visited them up there. Jehovah wants Little Mardie and Arie to be with him. He said we could all go and see them anytime."

Sriracha nodded. One small tear came to his eye. He wiped it away.

"May I have some coffee?" he asked.

"Sure. Sit down and I'll get it."

"May I smoke?"

"Considering the circumstances," Mili answered, "it's okay this one time."

Sriracha lit a cigarette as Mili served him a cup of black coffee. She fixed herself one too, full of cream and sugar, and a little coffee. She sat.

"How do you feel?" she asked her son.

He looked forlorn.

"Like I've been robbed," he said. "I saw Little Mardie at school every day and she always had something cool to say. Lately she'd call out what kind of chores would be waiting for me when she and Arie farmed their land. You can muck out the horse stalls, she'd say. Or, you can muck out the pig pens. Or, you can muck out the chicken coop."

"She never really would have made you do those things, would she have?" Mili asked.

"No, of course not," Sriracha said and smiled. "She was teasing. She knew that I am studying to be a graphic novelist, not a friggin' cow hand."

"There's more to farming and raising livestock than mucking, you know."

Sriracha shrugged and smoked his cigarette.

"Someday we'll go visit a rancher who I know down here. His name is Wyatt Earp.

Have you heard of him?"

"Nope," Sriracha answered with zero interest.

"Well, you will. When you get to the Wickett sisters' story about a secret Mormon settlement that was destroyed a long time ago down here."

Sriracha nodded without interest. Mili might as well have said someday you'll want to know more about medications for cholesterol and procedures for hip replacements. Right now, Sriracha was like every human teenager anywhere. Tomorrow was for excitement. Not for old folks' stories.

Jesus wandered in sleepy-eyed.

"Why is everyone up early?" he asked.

Mili patted her lap. Pint-sized ten-year-old Jesus sat and wrapped his arms around his mother's neck. She put her own arms around him and gently shared why she and Sriracha were up early.

✳ ✳ ✳

Russell Kruckenberg and Don Korpinen were smoking cigars together in Kruckenberg's duplex. Russell was thick and strong with a full head of salt-and-pepper hair. He wore a gray jumpsuit and Nikes. Korpinen was slim with mostly white hair. He liked to relax in slacks and a nice dress shirt. The two SEALs had served together and both had been decorated for missions in the Iraq wars. Don often joked that his medals were for humping ammo into a firefight, and that Russ's were for shooting it all off.

The men were concerned about the ongoing hunt by Arab shooters tracking SEALs in Hell. They sat with chips, beer, cigars, and their Ceska Sprojovka Uhersky assault rifles propped on the carpet and leaning against their knees. They had upgraded from their old Barrett REC7s when Arabs became interested in SEALs down here. They wanted Russian AK47s but could only get the Czech automatics. They were good enough for NATO and they would be good enough for them. Each thick black gun had a fresh rectangular magazine shoved into its breech with its bottom sticking out. Like Lego guns made for real soldiers.

They were watching an old video of then Commander-in-Chief George W. Bush landing on an aircraft carrier in a Lockheed Viking

99

military jet during the second Iraq War. He emerged from the cockpit wearing a flight suit and a pilot's helmet, grinning and waving.

"I love that son of a bitch!" Russ exclaimed.

Don nodded.

"A SEAL's best friend," he said. "If it hadn't been for him, you and I would've been doing practice missions on a simulator in Pensacola instead of sneaking into Baghdad. Would have been fun though if he'd landed on a hostile carrier by mistake."

"He'd have rolled with it," Russell declared confidently. "Russian ship? Vodka. Chinese ship? Tea. The man is flexible."

"Don't think he drank booze *or* tea," Don commented.

Russell grinned and watched Bush saluting the troops on the carrier. A loud ringing alarm suddenly sounded in the duplex. Both SEALs grabbed their rifles and hit the floor. Such alarms had been installed by Lucifer's technicians in every SEAL home after the Arab assassins had become active. They soundednytime anyone put their hand on the outside door knob. Kruckenberg waited for the door to be forced open. Korpinen just prayed that it would be. It wasn't.

Whoever had touched the doorknob proceeded to pour automatic weapon fire into the wooden door. The two SEALs inside returned fire and when the door sagged—shot to pieces—an explosion rocked the outside hall blowing wood and metal fragments into the living room. The two SEALs were protected behind the massive sofa. They crawled forward, weapons trained on the doorway. Two dead Arab soldiers lay in the hall. They had been blown to bits by a grenade that had gone live and then slipped out of the hands of the soldier who had pulled the pin. Kruckenberg and Korpinen inspected the dead men, relit their cigars, and waited for reinforcements to arrive.

✷ ✷ ✷

John Gilbert lived in a duplex two units away from Russell Kruckenberg's place. He heard the grenade explosion, knew what it was, and shouted to Milo Lyon who was pissing in the head.

"Milo, we got incoming!"

Gilbert and Lyon had served as SEALs after the second Iraq War. Gilbert had been a captain and Lyon was his company non-com. They had known Kruckenberg and Korpinen in the navy and beat them down to Hell when insurgents in Oman cut off their retreat from the Yemeni embassy right after they had concluded an unofficial visit to the ambassador, which had turned out to be fatal for him.

Lyon rushed out of the bathroom and he and Gilbert stormed down the duplex fire stairs carrying loaded Remington Bushmasters. They raced across the lawn toward Kruckenberg's place and spotted several armed Arab soldiers standing outside. Both Gilbert and Lyon dropped to the grass. One of the Arabs saw them and cried out to the others as he lifted up his rifle. The SEALs fired at them from less than twenty yards away. The four armed shooters were hit by such a storm of bullets that two men lost their heads, one had his body cut completely in half, and the last simply dropped in a bloody heap.

In moments, Russell Kruckenberg and Don Korpenin came out onto the duplex balcony guns ready and saw John Gilbert and Milo Lyon walking over to inspect the dead.

"We took out two up here!" Kruckenberg shouted. "How many down there?"

"Four," Lyon called out.

"We kicked their ass and took their gas!" Kruckenberg shouted. It was a time-honored SEAL mantra and was only uttered when victory had been sweet. "Take their weapons and come up here to my place. There are cold brews here at Kruckenberg's Acey-Deucey Club and six weapons to hide before we call this in."

Both Lyon and Gilbert grabbed the rifles scattered on the grass and ran like hell for the stairs up to Kruckenberg's place. Like so many residents before them, they could not imagine living anywhere else but Hell.

✳ ✳ ✳

Mili and Mardie were drinking piña coladas at noon in Mili's kitchen. Mardie sipped at hers and smiled mischievously at her twin.

"Tell me again why we're boozing it up during the lunch hour?" she asked.

Mili answered without looking at her.

"I ran out of coffee."

Mardie arched her eyebrow.

"But you had liquor and mix for piña coladas?"

"No. I had Pfot take me to Hells Bells. Then I sent him to pick you up."

"Unannounced," Mardie noted.

"I called you," Mili protested.

"In bed."

"You were awake."

"That's not the point," Mardie responded.

Mili looked her sister in the eyes.

"What exactly *is* the point, Mardell Wickett?" Mili said in an ornery tone.

Mardie gazed at her sister. Drinking early. Cranking over crap. Then she answered slowly.

"Are you sad today?"

"Yes," Mili admitted. "Am I acting like a bitch?"

"It's okay, Mil," Mardie replied slowly. "You've had a terrible loss."

"Both boys woke up early and wanted to know what was going on."

"You told them?"

Mili nodded.

"Talking about it made everything worse."

Mardie nodded. What was there to say to that? How do you deal with another person's tragedy after the fact? Never bring it up? Bring it up all the time? Another lesson she'd never learned in life. She drank down the last of the piña colada. *That* she knew how to do.

"Seconds?" Mili asked. Mardie nodded and handed her the empty glass. Mili rose and refilled it from a pitcher in the fridge.

"Where is that drink from?" Mardie asked. "Doesn't taste like SoHo or Chelsea."

"Nope," Mili answered. "It was invented in Puerto Rico. Rum, pineapple juice, coconut cream, condensed milk, blended with crushed ice. Might be able to get it at Crouch End or Muswell Hill."

"Where the rich Puerto Ricans live?"

Mili smiled a small smile.

"That's where the rich white blokes live who take their wives on cruises to Puerto Rico."

Mili put the fresh piña colada on the table in front of Mardie.

"Thank you," Mardie said. She looked at Mili. "Is some part of you thinking about when we might go looking for the kibbutz shooter?"

"I don't think about anything else."

"And?"

"And?" Mili repeated.

"And what are you thinking?" Mardie asked. "*Exactly.*"

"I am thinking that we should be seeing someone coming here to visit any moment now."

Company, Mardie wondered? Mili wore a summer dress and sandals. She was wearing red shorts, a white halter top, and flip-flops. Good enough for visitors unless it was Jehovah visiting on an off-television day.

"Who?" Mardie asked, just as someone knocked on the door.

"Come in," Mili called.

In moments, a Samn demon appeared in the kitchen doorway. Several of them had been assigned to guard the house with Arab assassins here, there, and everywhere.

"Excuse me, ma'am," the Samn said politely. "There is a Shapeshifter at the door who says that he has an appointment with you."

Mili nodded.

"Did he give his name?"

"Yes. He said it was Vladimir."

"How is he dressed?"

"He is wearing a black suit and the visage of Count Dracula of Transylvania."

Mili was amused.

"Vlad the Impaler?" she asked, referring to the Wallachian prince who had dispatched some twenty thousand captured Ottoman soldiers with sharpened posts. Pfotenhauer's demon connections had fingered the demon for selling Czech Ceska's and sent him to see Mili. He dealt in the kind of weapon that the killer had used at the kibbutz massacre.

Mili spoke to the Samn.

"Tell Vladimir that I want him to appear in his angelic form and to be prepared to reveal his true name."

"I'm not sure he will obey that, ma'am," the Samn replied sounding doubtful.

"Tell him it's either that, or I'll leave him in your hands."

The Samn smiled. Mili had never seen a Samn demon smile. It had rows of sharp teeth like a shark. Impressive. Mili wondered what it cost the Samn to have his teeth cleaned at the dentist. She supposed that depended on what it had been eating. Or who.

She studied the Samn for a moment.

"Do Samns ever bite someone during an *interrogation?*"

"It's been known to happen, ma'am," the Samn answered. "But not by me."

"You don't practice that technique?"

"I might someday, but not yet."

"Why the delay?" Mili asked.

"I'm waiting for Mike Tyson," the Samn replied with a straight face.

Mardie laughed out loud and even Mili grinned.

"Good luck with that," Mili told him. "Please convey my wishes to the Shapeshifter."

The Samn left only to return in a few moments.

"The angel's name is Magnanimous. He's a Power. He said that in his angelic form his gown will not fit. He is respectfully asking if Master Lucifer has a gown he might borrow.

"Tell him to come in here naked," Mardie told Mili. Her twin glared at her and responded to the Samn.

"Please wait and I'll see what I can find."

Mili got up and left to search Lucifer's closet in the master bedroom.

Mardie sat and grinned to herself. She'd seen a Samn's penis before. Never had seen a Power's member though. Probably wouldn't be that great though, all things considered. Otherwise, his angelic nomenclature would been Empowered.

CHAPTER TWELVE

Mili stood up when the Samn led the angel into the kitchen. He wore an old scarlet robe that Mardie had retrieved from Lucifer's closet. Magnanimous had blond hair and blue eyes. He bowed low from the waist toward Mili. Then he gave a somewhat perfunctory nod to Mardie. That irritated Mili. Prick thought he was better than her sister. Presumptuous to think it and stupid to show it.

"Sit, please," Mili told him a little stiffly. The angel didn't seem to notice Mili's tone. He sat and folded his arms. Mili sat and studied the fallen creature's demeanor. He appeared confident and comfortable. But folding his arms was a defensive gesture. It told her that Mr. Nonchalant was putting on a strong front. Which meant that he had something to hide and she knew what it was.

"You sell guns smuggled down here from Earth," Mili began.

"It is illegal to sell guns in Hell," the demon replied without emotion.

"But you do it."

Magnanimous nodded almost imperceptibly.

"I do. Lord Lucifer knows it. I pay his agents seventy-five percent of the retail price."

"And you specialize in automatic rifles manufactured in former Soviet Union satellite nations." The demon waited for her to go on. "Do you sell Polish FB Radom assault rifles?"

"They are very hard to move," the angel replied. "They're an acceptable weapon, but collectors prefer US and Russian automatic weapons."

"Collectors?" Mili asked.

"Yes. No Radom I've ever sold down here has been used to hurt anyone. Collectors *collect*. They don't shoot people."

"Wrong," Mili snapped. "A solitary gunman used a Radom to kill seventeen young people two days ago."

"No," the angel said confused.

"Yes," Mili said, now thoroughly angry. "He killed them on the Jewish kibbutz and the shells recovered at the site came from a Radom. *You* sold the gun to the murderer. I want the name of the *collector* who bought it."

"And what happens to me?" the demon struggled to say. He had turned completely fearful.

"I don't know and I don't care," Mili told him. "You're not the one I want."

"I will check my files and get you the name of the person who purchased it."

Mili stared at the gun dealer.

"Thank you, Magnanimous," she said in a tone that sounded anything but grateful. "One of the young people he killed was my daughter."

David Al-Din's name was texted to Mili by Magnanimous in twenty minutes. She called Lucifer who did not answer his mobile. Mili didn't know it, but her husband was through the rabbit hole destroying tanks and jet fighters. She called Michael Rockefeller.

"Hello, Mrs. Morningstar," he answered.

"Hello, Michael," she replied. "I have an urgent request. I need your help.Remember David Al Din? I want his address in New Babylonl. Remember David Al-Din? I want his address in New Babylon."

"I've only waited for you to ask," Michael told her. "South side of the city. Cutter Hall on Hanover Street. Apartment 307."

"Would you like me to inform Lord Lucifer as well?" Michael asked.

"Yes," Mili said. "I've tried to call him. He's busy. I've got my sister Mardie here. We'll talk and then I'll call you again."

"Right, ma'am," Michael replied.

Mili never called him back.

✳ ✳ ✳

Four Arab gunmen entered Avalon Lanes Bowling Alley. They were dressed in black jeans and black T-shirts and were bareheaded. Each man carried a Russian Kovrovskyi AEK-971 with extra magazines in their backpacks. The lead attacker shot two Samn demons who were stationed in the bowling alley watching the very wormhole the Arabs had just used to enter the alley. The team spread out and killed the bartender, the pin machine pixies, and eight people who were bowling. Then they raced out the front entrance breaking into two pairs, each pair knowing exactly where in Hell they were going.

A demon employed at Avalon Lanes had betrayed Lucifer's secret wormhole located there. The demon had gone to San Francisco and contacted the earthly demon network. He told them about the Avalon Lanes entrance to Hell and returned with a small leather bag full of high-grade diamonds. He had traded a lot of lives for those glamorous rocks. He didn't care.

Within a half hour, the information he sold was in the hands of the mastermind of the Arab invasion of Hell. He laughed, but no sound came out. His throat had been shot away and replaced with a mechanical voice implant. He didn't press the button to create a laughing sound. Feeling his chest wheeze in and out with satisfaction was enough. For now.

One pair of the Arab assassins ran through back streets of New Babylon toward the hills that rose beyond New Babylon. Millions of Hell's poorest residents dwelled in shanties on their steep sides. A GPS held by one of them showed the quickest way to the small brick-walled, tin-roofed, one-room building that the killers were targeting. Two SEALs lived in it, heroin users who had brought enough cash to Hell to stay mainlined for many, many years. Their names were Kenny Schermer and Eddie Kern. They were from Chicago. Both thought that living in Hell was a lot safer.

They had gotten hooked on heroin while stationed in Afghanistan, part of a team of SEALs that carried out weekly raids against the Taliban. They eventually dealt in the drug itself and were caught, court-martialed, and dishonorably discharged. They didn't care. Hooking up with a Saudi drug ring in Kabul they provided courier services transporting heroin from Afghanistan to New York. They used heroin, they delivered heroin, and they put away millions of dollars for a future with heroin.

The future dawned one winter day when they were discovered packing donkeys over the mountains from Afghanistan into Turkey. Kurdish irregulars—rebels against the government in Ankara—shot them dead and confiscated their heroin. The next stop was Hell where the two disgraced SEALs paid to have their money smuggled down by demons and then hid themselves in the endless ghettos above New Babylon.

The Arab assassins ran on narrow dirt paths through shantytown only stopping when the one holding the GPS held up his hand. Both assassins leveled their AEK-471s and fired into the doorway of a shack after the Arab in charge had kicked the door down. When they stopped shooting, the two men gazed into the makeshift house. It was filled with the corpses of small children who had been sleeping there.

The leader stared in frustration. He whispered only a single word. "Back." He turned and ran. His companion turned and ran behind him.

✳ ✳ ✳

Mili sat with Mardie at her sister's kitchen table. It was late afternoon and she had a cup of coffee in front of her and a dish of rocky road ice cream. The dessert was one of Mardie's favorites. Chocolate ice cream mixed with walnuts and diced up marshmallows. It had originated in America during the 1940s and had been marketed as a small bit of Heaven for those who had survived the Great Depression. Goodbye to *that* rocky road it beckoned. Mili nibbled at a spoonful.

She put her spoon down and reached in her purse. She pulled out her barrel-over-barrel Derringer and set it on the table.

"Tell me what you think you're doing," Mardie said.

Mili looked at her.

"I want to talk to the man who took Little Mardie from me." Mili's face was expressionless and her words were spoken without emotion.

Mardie understood her sister's grief. She knew what Mili was planning.

"What happens if you fail?" she asked.

Her twin frowned.

"Fail?" she repeated. "You mean what will I do if the shooter doesn't talk?"

Mardie nodded.

"That's why I'm bringing my gun," Mili said.

"You can also get killed, you know," Mardie reminded her.

"Yes," Mili agreed speaking slowly. "There is that."

"So why not just turn him in?"

"I want to talk to him," Mili repeated. "I want him to know what he did."

"You think you're the only one?"

"I'm the only one who knows where he is."

Mardie stared at Mili. Her sister stared back at her.

"When are you going to do this?"

"Now. Pfot is driving me."

"I'm going along."

Mili shook her head.

"You don't get a veto," Mardie told her. "I'm going with you."

Mili shook her head again but didn't argue. Mardie picked up her purse and pulled out her own Derringer.

"I've been packing ever since the assassins entered Hell," she told Mili. "Don't need some horny asshole deciding to take a break from hunting SEALs."

Mili smiled a thin smile.

"Piece of lead instead of a piece of ass."

"My thoughts exactly," Mardie replied and smiled herself.

"Finish your coffee," Mili told her. "I'm taking a pee. And then we're going."

Mardie drank down the last of her coffee and watched Mili walk out of the kitchen to use the restroom. She imagined standing outside David Al-Din's apartment and calling out to him that they just wanted to talk. Mardie hoped that he would look through the door peephole before shooting. She was pretty sure he would. What in the world could be threatening about two tall blondes knocking at your door? Would he suspect anything? Not as long as Jack the Ripper hadn't been his neighbor.

✳ ✳ ✳

The other pair of Arabs who'd entered Hell at Avalon Lanes were tracking down SEALs on the list to be executed. Four of the wanted men had been killed, but with heavy resistance occurring down here now, the remaining twenty targets would be harder and harder to take out.

Samn demons were everywhere and all of Hell's SEAL population seemed to be armed with automatic weapons and ready to defend themselves. As the killers made contact there was street fighting. Automatic rifle fire. Then grenades and mortars. There were armed SEALs and rooftop snipers everywhere. It made New Babylon seem like Damascus. Or Tripoli. Or Beirut. The Arabs didn't care. Neither did the SEALs.

High on the hills behind the city the pair of Arab assassins who had searched for the SEALs in the shantytown were now running headlong down the dirt streets back toward New Babylon. The ghetto was active with residents out looking to buy any food that might be available. They stepped off the roads and watched the Arab men dressed in black jeans and black.

T-shirts dash past them carrying their rifles pointed ahead of them.

Suddenly two men stepped into the road in front of the Arabs, raised their own rifles, and fired. In moments, both Arab shooters were down. Eddie Kern and Ken Schermer walked up to the dead assassins. They double-tapped the chests of the downed Arabs and put another dozen bullets in each body.

When the two SEALs were done, they exchanged high fives, said Bravo Zulu simultaneously, and headed back to their shack. It was far away from the one the Arabs had found. But they would only stay there a day or two more. It was prudent to move frequently with so many bullets flying around these days. They'd bought it together once before. They were making every effort for that not to happen again.

In New Babylon, armed Samn demons had surrounded the other pair of Arabs who had penetrated Hell. The assassins had hunkered down and so had the Samns. It would be a long night of battling, targeting lasers looking for prey.

Then two new Arab teams appeared from the Avalon Lanes wormhole. One pair was spotted by a squad of vigilante SEALs who shot them down before anyone had a chance to say salaam. The remaining Arab team entered the backyard of a home occupied by SEAL

Gary Holman. He'd grown up as a wheat farmer's son in Lamona, Washington. He joined the high school graduates who'd gone into the navy's special forces.

Nothing about dying worried him. His brother had fallen asleep driving a wheat combine during harvest and had been broken into a ragdoll by the voracious combine blades ripping through the wheat. His other brother had been killed when his light plane spraying the fields had clipped a power line and crashed. His father had died when he had slipped and fallen into the barn floor auger distributing wheat into lines filling grain dryers before silo storage. Smith knew that a farm could kill you just as fast as a hostile could. At least being a SEAL allowed you to give as good as you got. Most of the time.

One of the Arab assassins shot Holman through a window while he was heating up some canned pasta on the stove. He didn't feel a thing. His only real regret would have been that he not gotten to eat his SpaghettiOs.

CHAPTER THIRTEEN

Lucifer stood over his desk looking at a map of New Babylon. He had marked it with the known locations of the remaining assassins under siege in the city, two pairs of killers surrounded in different locations by armed Samn demons. The jihadists were holed up in residential neighborhoods and Satan was fearful of heavy Samn and civilian casualties if the demons tried to rush the Arabs.

Lucifer put in a secure call to the admiral who had earlier offered to deploy US SEALs in Hell to help exterminate the Arab shooters. He asked for and received a positive response concerning acquiring military drones to wipe out the two nests of assassins. The admiral told the Devil that he would provide drones and technicians to operate them.

With that done, Satan told Michael Rockefeller to bring him a BLT sandwich on wheat and two fingers of whiskey neat. Then he picked up his personal iPhone and called Mili.

"What's happening, doll?" he asked when she answered.

Mili tried to smile but failed.

"I'm having coffee with Mardie."

"Before dinner?" Lucifer asked surprised.

"Yes. We had piña coladas earlier. Coffee sort of cancels them out."

The Devil nodded.

"How are the boys?"

"They know about Little Mardie," Mili said quietly. "Sriracha got a call from one of his kibbutz classmates and he asked me what was going on. I told him and then I told Jesus. They are both sad but are counting on seeing Little Mardie and Arie up in Heaven." Mili paused and stared at her husband's face on her phone monitor. "Are you sure we will be able to see her?"

"Yes," Lucifer assured her. "Of course, we will. Right now, I'm up to my ass in Arab alligators, but as soon as things are under control, we'll head up to Heaven and visit Little Mardie and Arie."

"Today?" Mili asked hopefully.

"More like tomorrow or the next day," Satan answered. "But soon. Not sure what time I can come home tonight, so stay busy."

"No worries. We'll be spending a quiet night at home," Mili lied. Mili finished her call.

Mardie shook her head and wagged a finger at her.

A dozen drones arrived at Lucifer's headquarters, delivered by a team of Samns. They were accompanied by two South African nationals. They introduced themselves as freelance drone experts under contract to the US Navy. Both men were tall, black, and handsome. The Devil eyed them suspiciously.

"You're not Shapeshifters, are you?" he asked straight out.

"Not sure what those are," one of the South Africans answered in heavily accented English. "But we are holding genuine American green cards."

Lucifer smiled. Probably migrated to America on H1B visas doing jobs that could have gone to American technicians. His experience dealing with various military establishments around the world had taught him that every military hierarchy loved bringing in strings of foreign workers who worked cheap and were easy to dismiss.

The South Africans unboxed two of the drones. Each one measured roughly twelve inches across, with a pair of tong-like pincers beneath their wings to carry explosive charges. There were controllers to elevate, fly, unload, and land the drones. The flight controllers could manually release the bombs based on positioning instructions from ground observers.

Boxes of explosives the size of medium Amazon shipping cartons were brought forward. For all Lucifer knew, the explosives had been obtained from that online colossus. They had been opened and revealed clear-wrapped, orange-colored Semtex plastique explosives inside. The technicians attached one of the explosives to one of the drones' set of tongs and at Lucifer's nod, he elevated it and began to fly it toward the location where one of the Arab groups had dug in. Satan got the Samn on the phone who was commanding the demons surrounding the assassins' nest.

Lucifer put the Samn on speakerphone and listened as the demon spoke to the operator of the incoming drone, directing the South African to pilot it directly over the Arabs. The assassins saw it and immediately began firing their AEK-971s, but the drone was not hit. The operator released its bomb. It fell into the group of crouching Arabs and blew up everyone and everything.

The Samn on the speakerphone reported that the assassins had been liquidated. Satan heard the Samns there cheering. He asked the technicians to load and fly the second drone. The Devil called the Samn in charge at the other site where Arabs were holed up. He told the demon that a drone would be appearing shortly and his job was to make sure that the bomb was positioned precisely above where the besieged Arabs were entrenched. It came. It saw. It conquered.

As impressed as Lucifer was by the virtually instant destruction of both remaining Arab teams, the thought of using drones in Hell was profoundly disturbing. Those weapons in the wrong hands could take out his downtown headquarters. Or his home and family. Or the Ben-Yehuda Kibbutz.

He called Michael Rockefeller and reported the destruction of the assassins. He told Rockefeller to advertise the successful missions on the internet, and to post a single warning along with them that advised all of Hell's residents that any private procurement or attempted use of a drone would result in eternal life chained in Lucifer's office basement and fed only bread and water. Not all of Hell's good old days had been forgotten.

He also told Rockefeller to research who made the drones that had been used so effectively. He knew that the military had contracts with Boeing and Martin Marietta for long-range drones that seemed as big as military jets. But who produced these small bits of destructive genius for short-range use?

Rockefeller reported that drone commercial sales for the prior year were six billion dollars and were estimated to rise to twenty-three billion dollars by 2030. Quadrupling sales in a decade. The Devil told Michael to alert his top financial folks that he would be attempting to acquire all existing small drone manufacturers as well as buy out any promising ones in development. He wasn't going to allow them in Hell, but everyone else in the universe was going to have them. And they were going to buy them from him.

Mili had Pfotenhauer drive her to David Al-Din's apartment building. There were Samn demons and Navy SEALs everywhere. She could hear sporadic gunfire and then heard both of the drone blasts that Satan had used to end the current Arab threat. Pfot pulled into a visitor's parking space and Mili asked him to please wait.

"May I help in any way?" Pfotenhauer asked. He was extremely uncomfortable with dropping off the Wickett sisters in the middle of New Babylon's battle zone.

"No, Pfot," Mili told him. "We'll be fine despite the fireworks."

"I really think I should accompany you," Pfot insisted.

"Stay where we know we can find you," Mardie told him. "We might need you to carry a body for us."

Mili glared at her sister.

"She's just joking," she told Pfot. "Just stay here and we'll be back shortly. I am just interviewing someone about the kibbutz shooting."

Pfotenhauer stepped out of the Tesla and opened both passenger doors. He shut them after Mili and Mardie got out. He watched them walk up the sidewalk to the apartment building. Then he called Lucifer.

The sisters took the elevator to the third floor of Cutter Hall and found the door to 307. There wasn't a peephole in the door. Mili motioned Mardie back. She pressed the doorbell and stepped back herself. In a moment, the door opened a crack, then a few inches more. A young, Semitic-looking man peeked around the door. He wore black slacks and a white short-sleeve shirt. He saw Mili and Mardie and opened his door wide. He was not holding a weapon. Didn't mean he didn't have one tucked in his belt behind his back.

"Who are you?" he said in good English. His tone was polite.

"We are here to ask you about the shooting at the Ben-Yehuda Kibbutz two days ago."

The young man stood motionless.

"Why?" he finally asked.

Mili looked at the young man's face. He was not afraid. But he was anxious.

"May we come in, David?"

Al-Din was surprised that the woman at the door knew his name. He had not slept since the shooting at the kibbutz. It had weighed on his heart. So much so, that all he could think about was somehow escaping from what he had done. And now these women were here to ask him questions. He knew in his soul that he would tell them the truth no matter what the consequences.

Al-Din nodded.

"Come in."

The living room was furnished with a plain gray cloth sofa and armchairs on both sides covered in the same fabric. There was a coffee table, a big-screen television, and a red, black, and gray Oriental carpet that covered the center of the wooden floor. Mili and Mardie sat on the sofa. David sat on one of the chairs.

Mili got right to the point.

"Why did you shoot defenseless children?"

Al-Din shook his head and looked down.

"I wanted to punish the Jews who live there."

"Why? How had they ever hurt you?"

"They never hurt me," Al-Din said, speaking softly. "Their soldiers hurt me. They hurt my people. They attacked me and my neighbors when we protested Israel's policies. We were shot down in cold blood."

"So, you decided to slaughter Jews just as innocent as you were to pay Israel back?"

David nodded but did not speak. The woman hadn't spoken in anger. She had simply reminded him of the truth. He was a coward. A monster. A sinner whose misdeeds in Hell were even worse than his killing by the IDF soldiers in Bethlehem Square.

"I was wrong. All I could think of was taking advantage of the presence of all the Arabs invading Hell. I knew I could get revenge on the Jews in the kibbutz for what Israel had done to my people in Bethlehem and everyone would blame the Arabs." David looked at Mili. "But you didn't. Why?"

"The Arabs have blasted their way into Hell using *Russian* weapons. Plus, they are attacking US Navy SEALs. Not Jews. Your solo attack on the kibbutz tied to your use of a Polish automatic rifle made it possible to find you."

"But why did *you* come looking for me?"

"My husband is Lucifer. He and I have three children." Mili felt ill as she spoke, but she did not stop. "Our oldest daughter lived at the kibbutz and was taking classes in the high school. When you entered the classroom and opened fire, you killed sixteen of her friends, and you killed her. You killed my daughter."

Mardie started weeping softly. David looked at her and then he looked back at Mili.

He got off the sofa and fell to his knees.

"I am sorry. So terribly sorry. I have stolen a life from you. I have brought sorrow upon you and your family and shame upon myself and my people. I do not ask you to forgive me. What I did was unforgiveable."

Mili looked at him and then stood up.

"Where is your rifle?"

"Under my bed," Al-Din answered.

Mili walked into the adjoining bedroom. There was a double bed. Dirty clothes were stacked on one corner. Mili got down on a knee and looked under the bed. The automatic rifle was there. She reached for the weapon and slid it out. The thick black gun that had killed Little Mardie. It was hard for her to look at it and yet impossible to look away. She stood up with the gun. It weighed a lot.

She didn't know why, but that surprised her. It was a heavy, imposing weapon. Designed to elevate the riflemen who used them into some kind of super-soldiers. Odd how evolution taught soldiers to gauge superiority by such a thing. But it did. There were guns. And bigger guns. And the shooters who used them.

Mili knew that it would only take her Derringer to blow away the shooter who'd used this ultimate gun to murder her daughter. She walked back into the living room. Mardie watched her lean the rifle against the sofa and sit. She opened her purse. She reached inside and pulled out her Derringer.

David watched her without moving.

"Your grief will be somewhat lifted now that you have caught me," he told Mili. "It will disburse even more when you see me punished for my crime."

Mili frowned and grimaced. How could this monster understand anything about her feelings?

Suddenly David All-Din shot out of his chair and with one swift move grabbed the rifle from the sofa next to Mili. Before either of the Wickett sisters could react, he stuck the tip of the barrel in his mouth and pulled the trigger.

✳ ✳ ✳

Lucifer stood in David Al-Din's apartment with his arm around Mili's shoulders. He had received Pfotenhauer's call and had arrived only moments after the Palestinian shot himself with his own weapon. The back of his head had been blown out in a spray of blood and brains.

Dead, he dropped the rifle and fell backwards onto his sofa. He lay there with his mouth open and eyes staring. Mili told Satan who the dead man was. Satan regarded him with disdain. Mili regarded him with unexpected pity. And she noted inwardly that the man's self-inflicted death had indeed, as he had predicted, lifted a heavy burden from her heart.

Mili snapped pictures of his face and torso with her iPhone camera. She had no personal interest in the morbid documentation of David Al-Din's demise. She did, however, have plans to go to the kibbutz and meet with David Ben-Gurion and the parents of the high school children who Al-Din had murdered. Many of them would see this picture of his corpse and call it justice. Others would call it revenge. Mili called it climax and closure.

Did it make her less of a human being because her peace of mind had come only with the spilled blood of her daughter's killer? She didn't know. No matter how distanced she had remained from judging the murderers she had captured while with Scotland Yard, the only thing she had felt towards David Al-Din was bloodlust and the desire to see him destroyed for taking Little Mardie from her. Now he was dead. So, was she less human? No, she was a mother.

CHAPTER FOURTEEN

It was quiet in Hell. Lucifer sat in his office with his feet up on his desk. He turned his shoes one at a time and looked at the soles. No blood. That was a surprise, all things considered. It had been the worst week he'd ever experienced in Hell. SEALs had been assassinated. A dozen Arabs had been killed. Samns had been murdered. Citizens had been shot to death.

The hospital was full of wounded souls and the morgue was literally stacked with cadavers. His own daughter was dead. And sixteen other kibbutz kids were dead. He was as furious as he could ever remember being. He was amazed that he hadn't burned down his entire office building.

DNA tests had been run on the Arab cadavers. Every single one revealed Saudi Arabian lineage with signature western Asia, Negev desert, Yemeni, East Indian, and African sub-Saharan haplogroups.

Saudi Arabians, Satan thought unhappily. What the fuck? He could understand why there would be Arab retaliatory raids on Earth against Western military personnel. Christian soldiers had been killing Levantine Muslims ever since the Crusades. But this was the first time that Islamic warriors had entered Hell in search of retribution.

Goddamn wormholes. You can't live with them and you can't live without them.

The Devil picked up his desk phone and called Michael Rockefeller.

"Yes, sir," his assistant answered instantly.

"Emergency," he told him. "Two fingers of whiskey neat. ASAP."

"Yes, sir," Michael repeated.

Lucifer hung up.

Drinking in the middle of the day? Why not? He'd been watching folks get their livers shot out all week long. His still worked and it was time to appreciate that. Michael walked in with a Baccarat crystal tumbler and a bottle of Glen Fiddich. He put the glass on the desk and proceeded to fill it halfway. Satan nodded, picked it up, and drank it down. Michael refilled it without being asked. Lucifer nodded and let the whiskey sit.

"Thank you, Michael. You are the finest assistant I've ever had. And a real star preceded you. His name was Coogan. Gem of a fellow."

"What happened to him, sir?" Rockefeller asked.

"Got a hair up his ass that he could run Hell better than me."

"So, you fired him?"

"That, and a few other things."

Michael fell silent, truly afraid to ask what those other things might have been.

Lucifer looked at him, then he smiled.

"I'm not worried about you, Michael. You're a Rockefeller. You have many aspirations other than usurping my kingdom. Travel. Art. Philanthropy. All of them genteel and satisfying."

"Yes, they are," Michael responded. "But my biggest dream is that someday we will open a great museum down here."

"What would you call it?" Satan asked genuinely interested.

"The Metropolitan Museum of New Babylon."

The Devil nodded his approval.

"Plus," Michael went on, "many of the great artists throughout history are down here working, churning out masterpieces with nowhere to show them. Picasso, Calder, Pollack, Biddle, Benton, Rodin, Haring, Freud. Not to mention early Greek and Egyptian Christian artisans who haven't had a shot at a wall panel for thousands of years."

Lucifer smiled. He appreciated Michael's genuine enthusiasm.

"What about your famous interest in primitive art?" he couldn't help but ask.

"Somewhat diminished frankly," Michael answered. "Never been quite as fond of that stuff since New Guinea."

Satan nodded. Lost his taste for it, he thought ironically. His desk phone rang.

He reached for it.

"Speaking."

The office receptionist told him that a man had walked into the lobby and had asked to meet him. He identified himself as a United States Navy SEAL team commander with information as to the root cause and political source of the Arab attacks.

"Thanks. Michael is here. I'll send him down to escort him to my office."

Satan hung up and looked up at Michael.

"There is a senior SEAL officer waiting in the lobby," he answered. "Be a good lad and go fetch him, would you?" Michael nodded and left. "And bring another whiskey glass," Lucifer called after him. Michael gave a thumbs up as he went out the door.

The Devil could not imagine anything a SEAL could share with him that he hadn't already heard from the sailors fighting on Hell's different fronts. On the other hand, the SEALs he had spoken to had had little to say. They seemed bound up by a code that required action, not talk, and in almost every battle situation the SEALs had found themselves in, they had prevailed. Good on 'em. Dying didn't seem to be on anyone's mind. Killing was. Seeing the other side of a mission with their guns still in their hands was. Lucifer had never met a group of men so dedicated and so tough. He was impressed. Impressed indeed. And honored to have such men in Hell.

Michael led a tall man with thick, perfectly groomed black hair into his office. He was movie star handsome and had the bearing of a man who was confident with himself in any situation. He was dressed in khaki pants and a navy-colored Polo shirt. Lucifer still wore his clothes from last night, gray slacks and a blue-and-white striped long-sleeve dress shirt. He rose and came around his desk, extending his hand.

"Lucifer Morningstar," he said.

The sailor gave him a strong and friendly handshake.

"Commander Job W. Price," the SEAL said.

"Please sit, Commander," Satan told him, then signaled Rockefeller to set the extra whiskey glass down in front of Price. Michael did. Then he walked to the back corner of the Devil's office and waited.

Price sat in front of Lucifer's desk. He looked at the two glasses and the Glen Fiddich malt whiskey bottle beside them. He smiled. The Devil enjoyed seeing his smile and filled both glasses halfway. He picked one up and sat. He nodded at the other. Price picked it up.

"To life's conundrums," Satan said and held out his glass.

"May they all be solved with automatic weapons," Price said clinking Lucifer's glass. They both took a generous gulp.

"So why are you here, Commander?" Lucifer asked.

"I have not been involved in your effort to repel the Arab assassins who have breached Hell's sovereignty. However, I served as a SEAL for twenty-three years and a lot of that time I was in the Pakistan, Afghanistan, and other Islamic nations in the near East. May I share some impressions?"

"Absolutely," Satan replied. He lifted his glass towards Price, then finished off his whiskey. Price drank his down as well. Lucifer refilled both glasses. Price began. He was a polished and assured speaker, used to people listening to what he had to say.

"It is hard for some people to accept the fact that Arab peoples have regional looks—tribal looks—if you will. Yet Arab facial and corporeal features are uniquely stamped area by area, nation by nation, and are completely dominated by their ancient tribal roots. And, since Arab peoples very rarely intermarry, their looks have remained distinctive area by area. There is very little variation. Having said that, I viewed the dead insurgents' faces in the morgue and I would say without any hesitation that every one of the men are Saudis."

Price stopped speaking and looked at Lucifer.

Lucifer looked back.

"Saudi citizens?" he asked, knowing that Price was correct.

"I cannot tell that," the commander responded. "These agents could have been living anywhere. Saudis have the most extensive terrorist organization in the Mideast, with nationals located in every country, including Iran and Israel. However, because of the political support the Saudi royals receive from the United States government, they and their American ally deny the existence of that secret organization, and the clandestine missions they achieve, sending Saudi operatives to carry out spying, sabotage, and assassinations against Yemen, Turkey, Oman, Iran, Egypt, Algeria, Afghanistan, Kashmir, both India and Pakistan, Somalia, the Sudan, and even Indonesia."

"You can add Hell to your list," Satan told Price. "We ran DNA tests on the dead Arabs and you are correct. Every one of them mapped out with typical Saudi genomes." Price didn't speak. He was waiting to see where the Devil would take this.

"So, let me pick your brain, Commander," Lucifer went on. "Why are Saudi agents coming to Hell to track down SEALs? Life is life and when it's over, everybody passes into an afterlife. We have Jews and Christians down here in this one, drawing the wages of sin. I'd guess that's pay that most SEALs expect to receive when they die."

Price nodded silently. Satan went on.

"We have scores of SEALs down here whose earthly careers of murder and mayhem have long been over. Yet suddenly Arabs—Saudi Arabians we now know—are using wormholes to enter Hell for the express purpose of *killing* them." Lucifer scowled deeply. "I am not liking it."

"May I ask some questions?" Price responded. "Questions that may reveal motive and purpose?"

Satan nodded.

"I assume that you have checked earthly data bases for the identities of the dead shooters?" Price asked first.

The Devil nodded.

"We have, including the so-called ultra-secure databases of the United States, Russia, and NATO."

"Have you explored Saudi Arabia's databases, which contain top-secret files on both their spies and their special forces embedded in America, Iran, Israel, and all of its geographic neighbors?"

Lucifer frowned and took a drink of his whiskey.

"I don't recall receiving such information."

Price shrugged.

"Doesn't matter. Those databases are fake. A charade. The Saudis keep all of their *genuine* undercover activities logged in the US Central Intelligence Agency's computers. Finding those files would be almost impossible as theoretically they don't even exist. They're worth looking for, however, and they are real. They contain complete dossiers on every Saudi who ever served as a spy, saboteur, or bomber. Most of them are dead. However, some of those deceased Saudi agents have been reactivated and I believe that many of them have been deployed down here to assassinate Navy SEALs."

Lucifer sat completely stunned. He had never heard or even suspected that such a perverse activity was even possible. These Arab agents weren't just dead. They were *damned.* Judged and condemned to Islam's Hell, Jahannam. As removed as Jehovah was from the day-to-day activities of the various Heavens and Hells in the universe, could he really be ignorant of Hellion mercenaries being recruited from Muslim Hell to attack SEALs in Judeo-Christian Hell?

The Devil looked directly at Price.

"Sorry. What you're saying is impossible," he told him. "The Saudis cannot have their damned carrying on terrorist work."

Price pursed his lips and then smiled.

"And it wasn't possible that their agents were involved in the planning and destruction of the World Trade Buildings in New York City."

"They weren't," Satan protested.

"And it wasn't possible that the Saudi royalty knew that Osama bin Laden was actually hiding out in Pakistan and paid that government and its military leaders millions of dollars in hush money."

Lucifer shook his head slowly.

"There wasn't a single Saudi agent ever connected to the destruction of the Twin Towers, and no Saudi soldiers or operatives were encountered during the raid on Bin Laden's compound."

Price remained silent. He drank the last of his whiskey. Then he rose and spoke one last time.

"If you have genuine and truthful contacts at the CIA, use them to check on what I've told you. The Saudis *were* involved in 9/11. And they admired and protected Osama bin Laden to the very end of his life. He was a hero. He was a prophet. He was an enemy of the Christian West. And he was a Saudi. Check and contact me anytime."

Price wrote his cell phone number on a blank business card, bowed his head, and then followed Michael Rockefeller out of the office. Michael returned and Lucifer pointed at the chair where Commander Price had been. Rockefeller sat.

"First," Satan began, "have a background check run on Job Price. Was he really a SEAL? When did he serve? Where were his missions? And when did he wind up in Hell? Any and all of that information will be available in hacked files from the US Navy. Second, find out who our highest contacts are in the CIA. Look especially among the senior personnel running desks on the Mideast and Saudi in particular. Third, get me a copy of Seymour Hersh's book that claims to expose US fabrications about the raid on Osama bin Laden's compound. I read about it in an article in the *London Review of Books*." Lucifer gazed at Michael. "I think it's time I read it."

✳ ✳ ✳

Mili sat in David Ben-Gurion's living room. His wife Paula had served tea and raisin biscuits. David drank tea. Mili ate biscuits. She had showed Ben-Gurion the pictures of David Al-Din's corpse she had taken with her iPhone. Ben-Gurion had been horrified. A lifetime of tragedies had not managed to dull his emotional response to violent death.

"I don't think you should show those photographs to anyone on the kibbutz," he told Mili.

Paula was sitting on the sofa next to Mili. Mili reached over and held her iPhone out. Paula shook her head.

"I believe that you were courageous to go looking for that man," David told Mili, "and it must have been deeply affecting to watch him punish himself." Ben-Gurion spoke softly and looked at Mili. Mili looked back at him. "But the fact is that he *has been punished*. He is dead and can never hurt anyone again. Showing these sad pictures will not help anyone. The parents of the murdered children have already heard that Al-Din is dead. And they know that you brought about his demise. It's enough of an ending, Mili. Enough, as the Americans say, is enough."

Mili listened. But she wanted to show the dead face and the clumsy position of Al-Din's body fallen onto his own sofa. She wanted him to be mocked, to be hated, to be the object of derision by those who had lost their children to his gun. Was she so wrong to want that?

132

"I want the children to be avenged," she said. "I want their parents to see what happens when evil is confronted and destroyed."

David spoke.

"They *are* avenged, dear friend," he said. "And let me tell you, every Jew on this kibbutz has already had a lifetime of witnessing bloodshed and retribution. If there ever was a time to look to the future it is now. Your husband was right when he turned down my offer to field soldiers to fight the Arab assassins. He said he didn't want another Mideast here in Hell. Put your hatred away, Mili. It *cannot* be Jews versus Arabs here. It *cannot* be a world of crimes and retribution. It must be a new place. A place where peace can reign. Let us live in that world, Mili, not anywhere else."

Mili looked at David and his wife. She squeezed Paula's hand and looked again at the three pictures of her daughter's killer on her phone camera. Then, one at a time, she deleted them.

CHAPTER FIFTEEN

Lucifer sat as his desk drinking whiskey. Michael Rockefeller sat across from him drinking coffee. The Devil was reading the dossiers that Michael had brought him. Navy records on SEAL Job Price, and the Central Intelligence Agency's records on the Saudi assassins who'd been fingerprinted, DNA mapped, and photographed in the morgue.

"Price killed himself," Satan spoke out loud, eyes on his reading material.

"So, the evidence seems to suggest," Michael answered. "You'll note in the supplementary material included in the formal inquest, however, that many of his men, his fellow officers, and his mother and father strongly deny that he would shoot himself. If so, then who did? That's the question, isn't it?"

The Devil looked up and eyed Rockefeller.

"Are you being cheeky?" he asked.

"Never, sir," his aid replied instantly embarrassed. "It just seems unlikely that a man of courage and action would slip into his sleeping bag one night and shoot himself."

"He was depressed."

"He was a *SEAL*."

Lucifer nodded. Price had been found dead with a pistol in his hand inside a curtained berth at an officer's dorm in Afghanistan, and yet no one had heard a shot. Strange. Troubling.

"I went through the records on the Saudis," Satan went on. "Most had served in their military and many had direct connections with the CIA. They participated in Saudi missions all over the Middle East. I have to believe that the Saudi rulers knew about those involvements. Probably even ordered many of them.

"Another point. Every one of the Saudis in our morgue was killed in action on Earth. So, dear boy, are we not forced to admit that these dead soldiers were Hellions? And if so, then there is only one place where they could have been recruited and deployed."

"Jahannam," Michael answered. "Muslim Hell."

"Damned straight," Lucifer said vehemently. "Commander Price was correct about that. But how could *he* have known?"

"He learned it down here, sir. As you know, the information flashing around the demon network tends to be a harbinger of the realities discovered later by the rest of us."

"So, you're saying that Price has demon contacts?" Satan asked.

"Who doesn't?" Michael answered.

The Devil nodded and set the papers down.

"I'll deal with that shite in a minute," he said, and picked up a hardcover book. He held it out to Rockefeller. "Please read this."

Michael took it and studied the dustjacket. Then he looked at Lucifer.

"Seymour Hersh's take on the Osama bin Laden assassination?" he asked.

"Yes. He agrees with Price that the Saudis knew for years exactly where Bin Laden was hiding and held the information back from the Americans, even while they funneled millions of dollars to the Pakistani military and government to support him and his family.

Hersch couldn't even estimate how much hush money had been distributed as bribes. Despite all their efforts, however, someone betrayed Bin Laden.

"Hersh says that the US had a walk-in source who provided the information on Bin Laden's location and was paid $25 million for it. The highest levels of the American government confronted the Pakistanis and demanded cooperation in taking Bin Laden out. More money exchanged hands and you know the rest. The Saudis were left out of the loop."

Lucifer watched Rockefeller page through the Hersh book. When Michael looked up, the Devil asked him a question.

"Your opinion on how the pieces add up?"

"Taking the established facts *and* accepting Hersh's investigation at face value," Michael replied, "it appears that a Saudi presence has indeed recruited Hellion Saudi soldiers to enter Hell and punish the SEALs who carried out the raid on Osama bin Laden."

"Excellent," Lucifer said. "But how about a slightly more metaphysical version? A presence in Muslin Hell *itself* is actively recruiting Hellion followers to murder the SEALs who killed him and most of his family."

Rockefeller raised his eyebrows in surprise.

"Osama bin Laden himself?" Michael said.

Lucifer nodded.

"The evil that men do lives after them, and with enough money it just keeps on living. And at least one of my demons—aka fallen angels—is cooperating with Bin Laden."

"I don't understand, sir," Rockefeller said.

"A demon had to have revealed the existence of the wormhole at Avalon Lanes, which several jihadists used to enter Hell yesterday. It also dawned on me that that same demon may well have performed other acts of betrayal, including pinpointing a wormhole in Afghanistan near the barracks where the SEAL officers—including Commander Price—were quartered."

"Setting up Price's murder?"

"Exactly. Put out word to the demon network that I want the name of whoever among their peers sold the location of the Avalon Lanes wormhole to the assassins and/or the space gap used to murder Price. Reward in cash. Or bowling credits."

Satan went on.

"I also want you to ask a high-ranking Power or Dominion that *you* personally trust to go and check the proximity around the spot where Price was hit. He'll be searching for the wormhole that was used to kill Price. And here is the hard part. He has to enter it and see where it goes. Angels can see such holes. Humans cannot. Otherwise, I'd send you."

Michael grinned.

"You'd send me to Afghanistan?"

"Sure, I would," Lucifer replied. "Much safer than New Guinea."

Rockefeller laughed out loud.

The Devil smiled and drank his whiskey.

Mili came back to her home in New Babylon. Mardie hugged her and assured her that Sriracha and Jesus were fine, and as the kibbutz high school was re-opening tomorrow, Pfot had agreed to take Sriracha and Jesus back to the kibbutz. Sriracha was going to resume his sequential art course and Jesus wanted to play with his friends and write notes to them in Hebrew.

"The boys will be okay," Mardie assured her twin. "I called Moshe Dayan and he is happy to have both of them bunk at his place so you can stay here in town. I haven't heard anything from Lucifer since the last Arabs who infiltrated Hell were eliminated."

"I talked to him last night," Mili told her. "The two wormholes the assassins used are effectively closed."

"You can't close a space opening," Mardie reminded her.

"No," Mili acknowledged. "But you can move its opening. And the openings on both of the ones used by the assassins have been moved. To the bottom of Lake Pius XII."

"Didn't that used to be a lake of fire?" Mardie asked.

"Yes, and it was a place of punishment for the pope who refused to prevent Rome's Jews from being rounded up by Mussolini during World War II," Mili explained. "Lucifer authorized kibbutz workers to fill it in with fresh water after the wormholes were capped and moved there."

"And the pope?" Mardie asked.

"He's manning a new lifeguard station wearing a pair of Speedos."

Mardie chuckled.

"I didn't know that popes wore Speedos," she commented.

"I didn't know that popes even *owned* Speedos," Mili added. "How about some coffee?"

"Is it after five o'clock?"

"Would you rather have some wine?"

Mardie shook her head.

"No. I'd love to have coffee, but it keeps me awake if I drink it too late."

"How about some decaf?" Mili asked walking toward the kitchen.

"Oh, sure," Mardie said following her. "That's like getting a kiss through a screen door."

"What about a compromise?" Mili asked her. "I'll have coffee and *you* have wine."

Mardie grinned and nodded her approval.

"It's really a shame you aren't the secretary-general of the United Nations, Sis. You are a gifted negotiator."

"Ha!" Mili chuckled. "All things considered, I'd rather be a contender for the Nobel Peace Prize."

"Or the Nobel Coffee Prize."

"I'll take either one. They both pay the same."

Mili brewed coffee and served Mardie a glass of California chardonnay. She added cream and sugar to her coffee and sat at the kitchen table with her sister.

"I feel like cooking supper tonight," Mili said. "I could use a little domestic tranquility. What would you like to eat?"

"How about hot dogs?" Mardie suggested.

"I have some vegetarian meat in the freeze," Mili told her.

Mardie made a face.

"Vegetarian meat? Talk about a kiss through a screen door."

"It's ground round."

"So, it's Jesus's vegetarian meat? From animals who are vegetarian?"

"Yes."

"The boy is a delusionary genius. Someday he'll surely talk himself into dating widows who are virgins."

Mili laughed.

"Thanks for believing in him."

Mardie held out her empty glass.

"More wine," she said. "And get the vegetarian meat thawing."

✳ ✳ ✳

Lucifer picked up a call from Mili.

"Yes, my one and only," he answered.

"More like your one and lonely," she told him.

Satan looked at his wristwatch. It was only 3:30 p.m. Had Mili been drinking? He had. He looked at his own empty glass and motioned Rockefeller to fill it.

"I will make up for that, love," he told Mili.

"How about some BBQ at home tonight?" she asked.

"Deal," Lucifer replied. "Maybe some grilled corn on the cob, too?"

"Sure. Like that street food we had in Athens?"

"No. That was so dry I could hardly swallow. I'm thinking the corn we had in Mexico City. Brushed with olive oil."

"That *was* special," Mili said remembering. "I'll pick up some fresh corn up at Hells Bells."

"Thank you," Satan said. "And when we're together, I want to talk to you about our trip to Heaven to see Little Mardie."

"How wonderful!" Mili exclaimed.

"We can go tomorrow night. We'll take the boys. Mardie is invited, too."

"Oh, thank you!"

"You're welcome, love. And to be frank, we have to go anyway."

Mili frowned.

"Pardon me?"

"I have a meeting with Jehovah concerning the Arabs who have entered Hell," Lucifer said. "It should be an eye-opener for the Old Man. I asked that he invite Muhammad to be there, too."

Mili sat dumbstruck.

✳ ✳ ✳

Dinner was quiet, but happy. Mili made hamburgers, homemade French fries, and Mexican-style corn on the cob. Satan ate three cobs with his meal. Mardie smiled through dinner. Especially each time Mili filled her wine glass.

"The stack of evidence is in," Lucifer told the Wickett sisters. "I am no sleuth, but I did my homework and came up with some conclusions that I feel are compelling. First, DNA results show that the dead Arab assassins were all Saudi Arabians. Second, they were Hellions from Islamic Hell, Jahannam. Third, they were paid and dispatched by another damned Saudi, Osama bin Laden. He sent them after the Navy SEALs who assassinated him on May 2, 2011, almost a decade after he planned the destruction of the Twin Towers in New York."

"Overdue and well-deserved!" Mardie said vehemently.

The Devil nodded and gave Mardie a thumbs up.

"The son of a bitch is trying to revenge himself on the SEALs who found him and outsmarted him."

"And outshot him," Mardie added.

"Brilliant work," Mili told her husband. "The twists in this story offer surprises at every turn."

"Yes," Satan agreed. "But the facts clearly point to Osama and that's why I have to see Jehovah."

"Are you going to ask him to stop Bin Laden's activities?" Mili asked.

"It's more complicated than that, I'm afraid. Jehovah exercises a hands-off policy on the Heavens and Hells of every religion. He does not directly intervene in any of them, but he *will* let me appeal for help from Islam's greatest figure." Lucifer looked expectantly at Mili.

"Muhammad," she guessed.

"Yes. Muhammad's holy life and righteous teachings led Jehovah to grant him the spiritual rule of Jannah, Muslim Paradise. It is full of gardens and every kind of material abundance. Like Judeo-Christian Heaven there is no sorrow, hurt, fear, or shame, and everyone is eternally happy. Also like our Heaven and Hell, there are angels and jiins, but jiins are not fallen angels. They are separate entities who live on Earth as well as Heaven and Hell, able to bless or drive humans crazy."

"Sort of like kids," Mardie commented.

"Ha!" Satan chuckled. "The fact is, unlike our Hell, there are no children in Jahannam. Also, another important differentiator about Islamic Hell is that its sole purpose is to cleanse the damned so that they may go on to Heaven."

"What?" Mardie almost shouted. "Even Osama bin Laden?"

Satan shrugged.

"Why not?" he replied. "The Muslim Holy Book, the Qu'ran, explicitly teaches that at the end of time, Muslim Hell will be empty."

"Oh, my God," Mardie said.

"Not *your* God," Lucifer corrected her. "Jehovah expects that his Hell down here will be completely full when Earth is spent and has announced his intention more than once that it go on forever."

"But isn't he one and the same as Islam's Allah?"

"Yes, but he was greatly influenced by Muhammad's desires that God should be merciful. He granted Muhammad's request that Jahannam's purpose be not punishment, but salvation."

"So," Mili interrupted, ignoring her twin, "Muslim Hell is a place of spiritual counseling and divine tutoring?"

The Devil shook his head.

"Oh, my no," he answered. "It's full of fire and brimstone, whipping and cutting, hunger and thirst. It's as awful as any place in the universe. And it is ruled by one of the most dark-hearted beings that God ever created. He is the Archangel Maalik. Lover of torture, pain, and punishment."

Both Mili and Mardie frowned in consternation.

"And since I am going to ask Muhammad for permission to meet with Osama bin Laden in Jahannam," Lucifer finished, "I will have to deal with Maalik." A twisted smile appeared on Satan's lips. "Whoever wants to go with me will need to get out their sun block."

CHAPTER SIXTEEN

Lucifer led his family to the wormhole in his house. They stepped out in front of the marble and gold façade of Jehovah's great temple home. Archangel Michael was waiting in the outer courtyard to greet them. He waved and walked over. He introduced himself to Satan's two boys.

"My name is Michael," he said. "I work for God. What are your names?"

Sriracha shook Michael's hand.

"My name is Sriracha," he said.

"Ho, ho!" Michael declared smiling. "And are you a real hot guy?"

"I smoke," Sriracha answered. "Does that count?"

"Absolutely," Michael said grinning. "You know what they say. Where there's smoke there's fire. It's a pleasure to meet you, Sriracha. Is this your younger brother?"

"Yes," Sriracha answered. "But you won't believe his name."

The Devil glared at Sriracha.

Michael grinned.

"It's Jesus," Sriracha told him. "He's ten."

Jesus bowed his head politely and extended his hand. Michael shook it and admired the confident bearing of the littlest Morningstar.

"That's quite a name to live up to," Michael commented.

"So far so good," Jesus told him.

Michael laughed with delight.

"I like your attitude, Jesus Morningstar."

"And I like meeting another Archangel," Jesus told him. "Though I have seen you visiting my father before."

"I am a great admirer of his," Michael said. "And let me tell you, I have learned just how smart your mother and her sister are, too."

Michael walked over and shook hands with Mili and Mardie.

"I mean every word," he said smiling at Mili. "I'm still amazed that you figured out the whole sad tale of Gabriel's demise the last time you were here." He looked at Mardie. "Actually, the last time *you* were here was just a few days ago," he said and winked. "How's Charlton?"

"Every inch a man," Mardie said, then instantly flushed.

Lucifer and Mili laughed loudly.

Michael laughed and shook his head.

"All righty then," he said. "Jehovah is waiting for you. Let's head over."

"Has the other guest arrived?" Satan asked.

"Yes," Michael answered. "He came last night and had dinner with Jesus." He looked down at Lucifer's boy. "*Our* Jesus," he clarified. "They have quite a mutual admiration society. Muhammad has huge respect for Jesus's obedience to God, even unto death. Jesus, in turn, is proud to honor Muhammad as the prophet who succeeded him preaching God's grace and unconditional forgiveness."

"We heard about the Muslim underworld," Mardie said. "Where everyone receives a Get Out of Hell Free pass."

"I know," Michael said. "Isn't that the damnedest thing?"

"Can I transfer there?" Mardie asked.

"Don't think so," the Archangel replied and smiled. "Though you can always ask Jehovah."

Mili and Sriracha stared daggers at Mardie. Jesus looked hurt. Mardie shook her head to show that she was kidding.

Michael led everyone across the great outer courtyard of the temple, and through the gate into the smaller yet still ample inner courtyard that faced God's home. He opened the massive golden doors and shut them after everyone was inside. Mounted torches lit the long hall that led to Jehovah's great room.

A relaxed Jehovah sat on his divan facing his visitors. He was barefoot wearing a long white robe with sleeves that covered his arms. He had blond hair and looked like Brad Pitt again. Lucifer knew instantly that God was clearly dipping into the Oceans movies.

God stood up and welcomed his visitors.

"Mili, God loves you," he said and chuckled. "I mean it. I'm still marveling at how you and Agatha made things happen up here."

"Thank you, Lord," Mili said.

Before she or Satan could introduce the boys, Jehovah pointed towards the open doorway.

"Michael will take you to see Little Mardie while Lucifer and I talk biz." He waved his arm as if to say away you go. "Hug your sister for me, Sriracha and Jesus."

Jesus looked flabbergasted.

"You know our names?" he almost gasped.

"I'm God," Jehovah reminded him. "Remember?"

"Wow," Jesus said. "You really *do* know everything."

God shook his head and smiled.

"Well, between you and me, Jesus, not *everything*," he said. "But I do get the really important stuff right."

Michael took Mili and the boys. The Devil bowed deeply towards Jehovah.

"Thank you, Lord," he said earnestly.

Jehovah sat on the recliner and waved for Lucifer to grab a folding chair. Michael had brought in a pair of them for him and Muhammad. Jehovah opened the conversation.

"Rumors have it that this has been a terrible week for you," God said.

"Rumors?" Lucifer echoed.

"Demons," God explained. "Again, I am sorry that Little Mardie was taken from you. I know that you also lost citizens and a handful of Navy SEALS. I've already told the folks in Body Reboot to provide any replacement Hellions you request." Lucifer nodded his thanks. "And tell me now," Jehovah went on, "what is going on with Arabs invading Hell's turf?"

"They are Saudi Hellions, Almighty," Lucifer replied. "Agents from Jahannam recruited as mercenaries to attack certain SEALs in Hell."

Jehovah frowned deeply. The Devil could feel God's anger building.

"I am offended just by the thought of such a willful violation of eternal law." Jehovah stared at Lucifer as if weighing his veracity. "Who is the instigator?"

"I cannot prove it yet, Lord," Satan answered. "But the evidence strongly suggests that it is Osama bin Laden."

Jehovah pursed his lips and thought about that.

"I understand now why you asked to have Muhammad join us," God replied. "Bin Laden is under his colleague's purview, the Archangel Maalik. Bin Laden has been burning in Muslim Hell for ten years now, and I mean burning. Last I heard he was tied to a stake and the flames at his feet were stoked continually." God fell silent thinking about the implications of his description.

"Muhammad will know his status," Lucifer said. "I should tell you by the way, that my sister-in-law Mardie wouldn't mind being reassigned to Jahannam."

"Ha!" God chortled. "Because it doesn't last forever?"

"Exactly."

"You can blame that on Muhammad's soft heart. That tender son of a bitch never met a person he couldn't forgive. And he thinks I should be like that, too."

"Jesus isn't like that."

"No, he isn't. Kid is as tough as nails. Lived and died an ornery Jew. Never gave a flying you know what about the Gentiles."

The Devil couldn't help but grin. It was thanks to Paul of Tarsus' inventive genius Jesus had become the Christian Redeemer of billons of Gentiles throughout world history. Most of them wore gold crosses.

Jehovah stood up again and looked toward the entrance to his room. Muhammad Bin Abdullah bin Abdul Mutalib stood there. He was of medium height and weight. A handsome, ruddy-faced man, with red hair, a full copper-colored beard, and very fair skin. He wore a green turban, a white robe, and leather sandals.

The moment he saw Jehovah, he prostrated himself of the floor, his forehead touching it
as well. God walked over to the prophet whispering to Lucifer as he passed.

"You could learn some stuff from this guy."

Like what, Satan wondered? The humble pie dropdown? He shook his head. Maybe God was right though. He didn't really have much knowledge of Muhammad aside from anecdotal misinformation riding the waves of Western prejudice. He had married above his station by proposing to a rich older widow. He loved to hang around beauti-ful *younger* women. He was a wise and wealthy merchant. He liked grooming immaculately and dressing well. And as Satan had just seen for himself, the man was Bollywood handsome.

Even if all those things were accurate, they were hardly faults. Why then had Muhammad gotten such a sour reputation in America and Europe? Two reasons most likely. His bad rep had been created by Christians who thought that his Islamic teaching had encroached on their religion, many actually believing that he had created a false religion. There was also the fact that many of the world's most violent groups were Muslim. Honoring the prophet and then slaughtering Christians, Jews, and most frequently, other Muslims.

Jehovah touched Muhammad on the shoulder. The prophet got to his feet and much to Lucifer's amazement, God hugged him. The Devil had never seen Jehovah hug anyone. He patted Muhammad on the back and then holding his hand brought him over to meet Lucifer. Muhammad smiled kindly. Satan was stunned to realize that the prophet smelled like vanilla and jasmine. And it was not perfume. Not even his son Jesus smelled this good.

Muhammad looked Lucifer up and down. Then he gazed into his eyes.

"Dear friend," he said in a pleasant tenor voice. "You seem to be missing your horns and your tail."

Jehovah guffawed rudely and Muhammad smiled. Satan just stared. Was the prophet really such a hayseed?

Muhammad extended his hand.

"So sorry," he told the Devil. "I was only trying to make a funny. I must admit that I did not expect to see you so tall, so beautiful, and so…so…blond!" Muhammad's English was slightly accented, but perfectly spoken. Lucifer smiled and shook his hand. The prophet had a firm and very friendly handshake.

"Please sit, gentlemen," Jehovah said. Muhammad waited until the Devil had seated himself in a folding chair and then he took the one next to him.

"Coffee or tea?" Jehovah asked his guests.

"Coffee for me, please," Muhammad spoke up without hesitation. Satan was surprised.

"You drink coffee?" he questioned, sounding like a school child who had caught his teacher smoking.

Muhammad smiled and nodded.

"Yes," he answered. "Ever since I switched from being a Mormon to being a Muslim."

God roared with pleasure, and even Lucifer managed to smile. This guy was a bit of a character. Funny. Irreverent. Maybe a match for his own clever-tongued sister-in-law, Mardie. Was Muhammad in the market for another wife, he found himself wondering?

"I'd like coffee as well, please," Lucifer told God. The Almighty had never offered him a beverage before. He'd offered him grief for an eon or two, and when reaching the end of that road the Lord had assigned him Gabriel's old job of hearing and answering believers' prayers. He had found that task utterly exhausting.

The Devil could handle Hell and run a galactic business empire, but juggling believers' needs simultaneously with those other tasks was uber demanding. He had gained a new appreciation for the mega-church millionaire pastors who happily loved their parishioners while raking in their bucks. They deserved every dollar.

A very pretty little pixie flew in with a tray carrying two mugs of coffee. The Devil smiled. He loved pixies. Muhammad smiled approvingly and commented to Jehovah.

"Ah, just as it is recorded in the Book," he said, and then quoted the Bible. "You understand my thoughts are far off…" He had selected words from Psalm 139. "For there is not a word on my tongue, but behold, O Lord, you know it altogether."

God tilted his head a bit and looked at Muhammad.

"You mean because I had your coffee prepared the way you like?"

Muhammad bowed his head deeply.

Jehovah smiled.

"I accept your homage, Muhammad Bin Abdullah," God replied happily.

The pixie flew over to Muhammad and handed him his coffee.

"What is this?" the prophet exclaimed surprised. "There is milk in my coffee! Quite dangerous for a man who is lactose intolerant."

"Oops," God said. "Sorry about that. I think I told her to put in sugar, too."

"Take my coffee," Lucifer told Muhammad. "I don't mind milk."

Muhammad thanked Satan and handed him the coffee with milk. The pixie then handed him the Devil's coffee without milk. It was black as coal.

Muhammad looked at it. Sniffed at it. Then he took a small taste. He looked at Jehovah.

"Why, ar-Rahman," he asked, calling Allah by one of his nine-ty-nine sacred names, "do you insist on buying cheap coffee beans?"

God sat up straight on his divan and protested.

"Those beans were not cheap!"

"Well, Most Gracious, they are not *good*."

God wrinkled his forehead.

"I bought the best Arabica beans available."

Muhammad gave a gentle nod.

"Available from whom?"

Jehovah looked at Lucifer.

"From one of *your* merchants, Morningstar."

Muhammad chuckled.

"Nicely done, Master Lucifer. Overcharging Allah himself and then giving him inferior beans. But I can remedy that with a caravan of the best Arabica coffee beans."

Satan was both embarrassed and oddly charmed by Muhammad's forthright manners. Too bad he probably still moved goods around the cosmos using camels.

"I will have fresh beans brought to a transport hole this very day," Muhammad promised. "Tell your angels to look for five white Land Rovers, each carrying bags of coffee secured to their rooftop luggage racks."

Jehovah nodded. He noticed that Muhammad had set his coffee down. The Devil drank his without issues.

"And how exactly is *your* coffee?" Muhammad asked him.

"Don't know," Satan replied. "The milk and sugar completely cover up its taste."

"And you are willing to drink it that way?" Muhammad asked amazed.

"I don't drink coffee for the taste. I like the caffeine."

Jehovah and Muhammad both laughed.

"Ah," Muhammad declared. "I can see that you, too, have trans-ferred out of the Mormon church." His eyes twinkled.

Lucifer nodded, keeping a straight face.

"Yes, I did."

"And what do you call yourself now?" the prophet asked.

"I call myself a husband dedicated to making his wife happy."

Muhammad clapped his hands with delight.

"I belong to that club myself," he said. "In fact, I carry several memberships."

CHAPTER SEVENTEEN

Mili hugged Little Mardie with her arms around Sriracha and Jesus and her sister Mardie as well. Family hug. Mili was crying and Little Mardie wiped her eyes. At last, everyone stepped back, hardly able to believe that the Morningstars had reunited in Heaven. Who would ever have imagined that the first family of Hell would be *here?*

Mili looked at her daughter. Her face was beautiful, her hair gorgeous, and her smile was happy. She was wearing an Alice blue gown over a white short-sleeve shell underneath the top straps. She wore glossy black patent leather shoes.

"And how are you, sweetheart?" Mili asked.

"Fine, Mother," Little Mardie assured her. "Where is Dad?"

"He's meeting with Jehovah. We've had some serious troubles in Hell."

Little Mardie nodded.

"The angels up here can hardly talk about anything but Arab killers stalking Navy SEALs."

"They surprised us at first," her Aunt Mardie told her, "but the SEALs pulled together and retaliated. There are probably four dozen dead Arabs now, compared to a dozen SEALs."

Mili spoke then and told Little Mardie the news on her heart.

"The person who hurt you and Arie and the other young people at the kibbutz killed himself."

Little Mardie nodded and shut her eyes for a moment.

"I want to come back home with you and Daddy."

Mili teared up again.

"What about Arie?" she asked.

"He feels the same as I do," Little Mardie said urgently. "Our lives were stolen from us. Our families were stolen from us. Why can't we just go back?" Little Mardie implored her mother with sad and desperate eyes.

"For now, I have to tell you that we've asked God and he is intent on keeping you and Arie in Heaven."

"Because he doesn't know how cool Hell has become," Sriracha declared. "I'll bet you anything."

Mardie touched Sriracha's lips with her forefinger.

"Let's not give Great Jehovah any clues, honey," his mother told him. Sriracha nodded.

Little Mardie took Mili's hand.

"Mom, I miss my friends, and the orchards, and the land Arie and I were going to homestead. Please, please figure out how to get us home." Little Mardie looked into her mother's eyes. "Please promise me. Oh, please promise me!"

Mili took Little Mardie into her arms again and whispered assurances that she would do everything she could to get God's permission for her and Arie to come back home. As she was holding her daughter, she could feel irregularities in her back. She carefully felt her way up and down Little Mardie's spine. Gunshot holes had been left in her Heavenly body.

"What is going on here?" she whispered to Little Mardie.

"I don't know, Mom," her daughter answered. "Three bullet wounds were left in my back. I don't know why."

When Mili had first entered Heaven, she had been given a saintly body, but with a foot missing that she'd lost to diabetes while dying. And now Little Mardie had three holes in her back as a lasting reminder of the terror and slaughter that had swallowed her and Arie at the kibbutz. Mili was furious. Whatever it took, she was getting Little Mardie and her fiancé out of Heaven. The wounds in her young girl's back had just reminded her that God was disfigured as well. He obviously had no heart.

✳ ✳ ✳

"Explain to Muhammad why you asked for this meeting," Jehovah told Lucifer.

"Muhammad," Satan began, "as strange and impossible as it may seem, I have clear evidence that Hellion assassins from the realm of Jahannam entered Judeo-Christian Hell and murdered several military men."

Muhammad looked stunned. Then sad and anxious.

"I thought that was impossible. How can it be true?"

"The Hellions were identified as deceased Saudi Arabian secret agents who accessed space wormholes to enter our Hell. We don't know how they found those passages, but at least two different locations were used. Those openings have now been moved and that has apparently stopped the assassins' ingress."

"Have you identified the guiding force behind this warped jihad?" the prophet asked.

"Yes. Our research on the American special forces men who were murdered in Hell—all Navy SEALs—revealed that every one of them was involved in the clandestine raid ten years ago that trapped and executed the founder and leader of Al-Qaeda, Osama bin Laden."

Muhammad's face fell. He looked down and did not speak.

The Devil continued.

"Our fear is that Bin Laden is behind the vendetta and we are not equipped to stop it. We can only respond to new attacks and that means that more SEALs will die."

Muhammad lifted his head. He looked miserable.

"I cannot imagine how I can stop Osama bin Laden either," he said, obviously feeling powerless.

God wasn't feeling powerless. He spoke with his half-Nelson voice. **"I say kill him right now and destroy his DNA record."**

Muhammad looked shocked and horrified.

"Who would ever do that to one of Allah's creatures?" he cried, truly alarmed.

Jehovah and Lucifer looked directly at each. Who indeed?

"Oh, please," Muhammad implored. "There must be another way. Jahannam was created by the all-merciful Allah so that even the most damaged of his children could be redeemed, changed, and forgiven. Jahannam is but the path to Jannah, Muslim Heaven. Who am I to deprive *any* soul of an eternity in paradise?"

It was clear to Satan that Allah had to be someone different than Jehovah. Redemption for the worst of the damned? Forgiveness for the likes of Osama bin Laden? The Devil felt disturbed to the depths of his perceptions of reality and God's control of it. Muhammad was sounding a lot more patient than Jesus, who advised his disciples to turn their backs on those who rejected his salvation shaking the dust off their sandals on the way out of town.

Was it possible that Muhammad had somehow been able to touch a remaining part of Elohim trapped deep within Jehovah? Had he somehow managed to awaken the God's grace allowing him to show mercy empowered by Muhammad's own righteousness? There was no other explanation. Food for thought. For later. Right now, he had to get Osama bin Laden under control.

"I like Jehovah's idea," Lucifer said. "The one where we kill Bin Laden and toss out his DNA."

Muhammad shook his head.

"Let us try and reason with Bin Laden," the prophet offered instead. "He needs to understand that what he is doing is wrong."

Nuh-uh, the Devil thought. If Osama understands anything, he understands evil. He was the mastermind who planned the murder of three thousand innocent civilians in the attack on New York's Twin Towers. And celebrated it in videos. Satan wanted to go back to kill Osama and flush his genomes choice again.

However, Muhammad was on a tangent of his own.

"If Bin Laden is informed that his revenge will only add hundreds, even thousands, of years to his torments in Jahannam, he may see that leaving off the vendetta is his best hope for release."

"What kind of torments?" Lucifer asked. Criminals in his Hell with adequate disposable wealth suffered no worse a torment than having to drink sparkling mineral water gone flat.

"Osama is in a great fiery pit," Muhammad said, "suffocating from smoke, frying in fire, and crying out for mercy as his skin burns off."

Satan turned pale. My God, *that* was a real Hell. If Bin Laden could somehow be promised to be freed from such agony, he might indeed be open to Muhammad's intervention.

Jehovah watched the Devil.

"Are you all right?" he asked. "You look queasy. Isn't Jahannam just like your Hell?"

"It absolutely is," Lucifer lied. He hadn't realized how long it had been since God had paid a personal visit to Hell. A lot had happened there. The skies were blue. The sun shined every day. Water was pure and fresh. Vegetables, grains, and meat were plentiful. So were Starbucks coffee stores and Ben and Jerry's Ice Cream shops. "Jahannam is exactly like my Hell," Satan told God again. The wages of sin were death, and a double scoop of Jerry Garcia.

Muhammad stood up.

"We can step into Jahannam using the same passage I used to come here. It is located in the outer courtyard and Archangel Michael can take us directly to it."

"All right," Jehovah said. "I am expecting you two to return with a solution that will return Hell to the peaceful place of suffering that Jahannam is."

"Lord," Lucifer responded, "it is important that Mili and Mardie be allowed to come with us. As you know their deductive powers would be helpful in analyzing and positing a truce with Bin Laden."

"Permission granted," God said. He knew the value the Wickett sisters would bring to the negotiations with Osama. He sent an angel to fetch them from where they were visiting with Little Mardie and Arie.

Muhammad bowed low. The Devil nodded. He had one urgent piece of business to conduct before he could leave. There had to be a place to take a piss somewhere around here. He excused himself and stepped out of Jehovah's great room. He found Michael standing outside of the opened doors of the temple. He turned and looked at Satan as he came out.

"Is there a men's room around here?" Lucifer asked.

"Back inside," Michael said. "Turn left. It's my private head, but you're welcome to use it."

"Obliged, Michael," Satan told him gratefully. "I also need a gun. What can you do for me?"

"A gun?" the Archangel repeated and arched an eyebrow. "For what purpose?"

"Jehovah is allowing me to accompany Muhammad to Jahannam to negotiate with Osama bin Laden."

Michael whistled.

"Negotiate? As in *kill* him?" he asked.

"Depends on what kind of gun you can find for me," Lucifer answered.

Michael nodded.

"Take your piss and I'll have a US-made Ruger 9mm pistol for you when you come back."

The Devil nodded. God bless America.

✳ ✳ ✳

When Mili and Mardie arrived, Lucifer took them aside to speak privately for a moment.

"Ladies, we are about to be escorted by Muhammad to Jahannam to speak with Osama bin Laden. I would very much appreciate your company and your help in negotiating with Bin Laden."

Mili nodded. Mardie stood silently.

"Thank you, love," Satan told Mili. He looked at Mardie.

"Are you okay to come?"

"Yes."

"I have to tell you that Arab Hell will be hot and fiery. Osama himself is subject to terrible suffering."

"I'm ready to come," Mardie said. "But maybe not transfer there after all."

Muhammad stepped off a stone pavement in the outer courtyard and into a slit in space. The Devil saw the opening clearly. Entering it reminded him of stepping between stage curtains. An invitation to disappear and reappear somewhere else in the universe. In this case, Muslim Hell. A Hell of a Hell as Muhammad had described it.

Lucifer stepped out of the wormhole. It was so dark and so hot that it made him feel faint. He couldn't see anything, and it felt like he had entered a gigantic cave, close and unbearably warm. Mili took his hand and Mardie took hers.

"Your eyes will get used to this place very quickly," Muhammad told them. "Look into the distance. That is where we are heading."

There was a red glow on the horizon. Muhammad led them toward it. Satan heard the sounds of human misery. Moans. Weeping. Cries of fear. Screams of agony. It made his skin crawl. Dear God, what was he doing here? Small pits began to appear. Holes in the ground that held a single damned soul. Their faces were on fire. Their hair was on fire. They cried out for mercy when they saw Muhammed and reached desperate hands toward him. Hands that were on fire. Smoke wafted out of the pits while the captives cried in terror and pain. Then he smelled the aroma of roasting meat. The humans in the pits were being cooked.

Muhammad walked on. Lucifer could see that the distant red glow had now enlarged into a red sky over their heads. Its origin was an endless lake of fire in front of him, its surface consumed by countless patches of fire—blobs of napalm glowing and burning. The Devil was filled with dread when he realized that every napalm fire encompassed a person or a group of people. Mili gasped and Mardie began sobbing. The damned were on fire, flames shooting up from their burning bodies. And they were screaming. Endless howls of affliction and cries for relief, begging Muhammad who stood on the shore surveying the endless bonfires of punishment.

Lucifer and the Wickett sisters stood next to the prophet. Muhammad himself was weeping hard, gasping for breath, and groaning at what he saw.

"How can you allow this?" Mili demanded.

Muhammad shook his head and didn't answer.

Mili's ears were filled with sounds of anguish. How would she ever get those cries of pain and suffering out of her ears? Out of her memory? This realm of punishment was beyond imagining, yet it existed. It was real. What did this place say about God? About Jehovah? About Allah?

Mili spoke to Muhammad.

"I don't think I can do this."

"We are close. I will send an angel to fetch Osama bin Laden from the lake of fire."

Mili felt faint and weak. Mardie's desperate hand clutched her shoulder. It was so hot, so close, so horrifying. She watched an angel appear and bow to Muhammad. Lucifer knew who it was. The angel made eye contact with Satan and recognized him as well. It was one of the Devil's most ancient adversaries. The angel's name was Maalik. He was a powerful Throne who had fought against Lucifer and his rebels. He was tall and swarthy with short black hair. He was wearing a black robe and sandals. Maalik stared at Satan, then he walked out onto the lake of fire.

In moments, he returned escorting a person who was tall, thin, and naked. It was too dark for Lucifer to make out the man's features. Maalik took the man to Muhammad and disappeared. The Hellion who'd been escorted bowed low from the waist to the prophet, then stood up and pressed a hand against the side of his throat. He used a mechanical voice to greet Muhammad.

"As-salam 'alaykum," he said. Peace be upon you.

Muhammad bowed his head.

"Wa 'alaykums-salam," the prophet replied. And upon you be peace.

Mili, Mardie, and Satan stared at the man. It was impossible to distinguish any features on his face. It was mashed, distorted, and shapeless. Only slowly did they realize that the Hellion's entire face and body had been damaged by bullet wounds. There were countless holes in his face and his chest, his stomach, arms, and legs. The top of his forehead had been shot off, leaving a gaping hole in his skull. Muscles were shredded and hanging loose. Bones had been destroyed, their sharp breaks erupting from the man's thighs, feet, hands, and chest. There was no blood, but all that did was to make this man's body look like a papier-mâché mockery of the real thing.

Muhammad turned to the Devil and held out a hand toward the spectre standing silently observing them.

"Lucifer, meet Osama bin Laden bin Awad bin Laden."

Bin Laden bowed slightly. Despite this ruined appearance, Osama bin Laden's Hellion body was alive, looking exactly like his cadaver after the SEALs who had captured him emptied their automatic rifles into his body. He reached up and used a hand to activate his artificial voice.

"As-salam 'alaykum," he said.

The Devil couldn't respond. There was no peace in this place.

CHAPTER EIGHTEEN

Muhammad turned to Bin Laden and returned his greeting for Lucifer.

"Wa 'alaykums-salam," the prophet told him. Muhammad stepped up to the motionless figure and put his hand on its shoulder.

"How are you, my son?" he asked tenderly.

Bin Laden pressed his mechanical voice box. The robot-like monotone spoke like the unworldly phantom he appeared to be.

"I am in great pain, Prophet Muhammad," Bin Laden spoke slowly. "Greater pain than I thought I could ever bear."

"It will not endure forever," Muhammad replied. "This is the Archangel Lucifer. He has reported to me that you are sending assassins into Christian Hell to kill the American soldiers who took your life."

"It is true. The fire of revenge burns as deeply in my soul as the fire of Jahannam burns my flesh."

"Dear Osama, that is vain," Muhammad warned. "All you will accomplish is to prevent your heart from being cleansed and released from this place of pain and suffering. What say ye to that?"

"I have no words, Holy One. Imagine my shock when I first came to this place. I had always seen myself as a hero of Islam. But awaking in

Jahannam after I died, I knew myself to be an *enemy* of Islam. The truth crushed my heart. But over time—even though I knew that I was being punished for being a detriment to peace and happiness in the human world—I grew so weary of inhabiting this pitiful wreck of a body that I began to desire to inflict pain and death on the men who did this to me."

"And you have," Lucifer interrupted.

"I have," Bin Laden readily confessed. "The men who left here to enter your realm are my brothers. They went willingly to destroy the US sailors who killed my son, shot my wife, murdered me in cold blood, and hideously mutilated my body."

Mili shook her head and gave a sharp rebuttal.

"Your Saudi Hellions murdered four of the SEALs who tracked you down, but they have also cost the lives of dozens of the Saudis you sent and a score of innocent bystanders as well."

"Those men are heroes," Bin Laden said. "The ones who have given their lives serving me have surely been resurrected to Paradise."

Muhammad shook his head.

"No. They are back here in the lake of fire, Osama. Just like you."

A deep groan emerged from the depths of Bin Laden's body. Its sadness was so profound that it made Satan's skin crawl.

Muhammad addressed Bin Laden's grief over the fate of his Saudi followers.

"This can stop, Osama," he said. "You need to comprehend that the violence you reap weighs down your soul with sin. Continue your hate-filled vendetta and you may well be the last Muslim to ever leave this place. Is that truly what you want?"

Bin Laden did not answer for a long time. Then he reached up and pressed his voice box.

"Great Prophet," he said. "I need time to think. If I give up this jihad, I will have nothing."

"If you give this up, this *sin*, my son," Muhammad told him gently, "you will have a clean heart and a peaceful soul."

Osama nodded but said no more. He bowed to the prophet and turned toward the lake of fire. He shuffled slowly back to the only thing he knew. Eternal fire. As Lucifer, Mili, and Mardie watched, Bin Laden's arms and chest caught on fire. Then his face and hands. The Devil turned away.

So, what had this visit accomplished, he wondered? Osama bin Laden's appearance voided any claims the SEALs might have had that they had done a professional job taking out the master terrorist. The only person telling the truth about the US raid on Bin Laden was Seymour Hersh. Bin Laden's body had been destroyed by hundreds of bullets, and likely not buried at sea, either. Had his corpse been tossed into the ocean for the fish to eat? Or hastily buried on Bin Laden's own compound without a word or a prayer?

Of course, Osama had brought it all on himself. But that didn't mitigate the cruelty of the way he had been assassinated, and the extreme disfigurement of his body. Why had his Hellion body been created to reveal the hundreds of shots fired into his corpse? His suffering in Jahannam was a given since Bin Laden was a Muslim, but being forced to spend the endless millennia ahead in this defaced and gory body seemed completely heartless.

"Does Jehovah know that Bin Laden's Hellion is hideous?" he asked Muhammad.

The prophet nodded.

"He decreed it, my friend. Only Heaven provides the dead with their eternal bodies as you well know."

"What now?" Lucifer asked.

"We give Bin Laden time to think."

"And if he says no?"

"Then we will ask God to help."

"God doesn't like to help," Mardie commented.

"I think he prefers that we work out things without always forcing him to intervene," Muhammad answered her. "In which case we shall ourselves find some loving way to deal with Osama."

Mili nodded. Lucifer thought silently that his own loving way might boil down to returning here and putting all fifteen bullets from the Ruger that Michael had lent him into Bin Laden's temple. Maybe that was an overreaction. A dozen bullets would probably be more than enough.

✳ ✳ ✳

Chuck Boyk was asleep in his Murphy bed. It was as narrow as a cot and its metal springs were covered by only a thin mattress. It was hard. Just like him. He'd been on over two hundred missions as a Navy SEAL, mostly working with Kurds in northern Iraq targeting unfriendlies in Baghdad, Ankara, Damascus, and Sanaa. His most important and exciting mission had been his participation in the raid on Osama bin Laden's compound.

His role had not been spectacular—not having been designated as one of the SEALs who shot Bin Laden's brains out—but his assignment had been significant. When one of the two Blackhawk helicopters crash landed at the destination, he and three other SEALs had stripped out secret stealth flight systems that involved presence reduction technologies, and then blew it up as the rest of the task force was being evacuated by the remaining Blackhawk. He never had talked about that mission and most people in Hell had no idea of his involvement in the most famous SEAL mission ever.

He slept with an AEK-971 these days. In the last few days, a lot of the men he had known and worked with in the Middle East had been ambushed and killed. Dyn Suchland. Jim Elliot. Forey Walter. Greg Smith. Steve Lightbody. Gary Holman. Further, others whom he only knew by reputation had been murdered. Bill Iverson, Jon Symonds, and Bob Tanke. All of them among the best SEALs who had ever served.

Other colleagues had been prepared for the attacks, like Don Korpinen and Russell Kruckenberg, and they had survived. In fact, they'd teamed up with other surviving SEALs and had taken down several Arab squads. Russ had personally brought Boyk the AEK-971 he now had, as well as extra rounds of ammunition he had taken off a dead assassin, telling Chuck that the former owner had been retired.

Boyk was lying on his back, fully dressed in his khakis and boots. He was resting, but he was not asleep. He took his glasses off for a moment and rubbed the bridge of his nose. He heard the front door to his apartment open. He had disabled the alarm. He grabbed his rifle but didn't fire. He wasn't about to blindly shoot at whoever set off the alarm. He wanted to see the actual perp and nail him as he tried to enter his apartment.

Boyk rolled off his bed onto the floor and looked through his bedroom doorway. He saw two men entering his home with rifles leveled. They were Arab men, bareheaded and wearing black T-shirts and black jeans. He shot round after round into the two men from his Russian automatic rifle. He rose to his feet and walked over to look at the dead men. Owe you one, Russ.

Mili, Mardie, and Lucifer were talking. And drinking. All three had arrived back at the Morningstar home bringing back Sriracha and Jesus from their visit with Little Mardie and Arie in Heaven. Mili was preparing a Thai chicken pasta for dinner, a meal that everyone loved. Mostly. Satan and Mardie always liked it a little less spicy. Sriracha wanted it hotter. Jesus never mentioned a preference but ate what he was served. As long as the chickens were vegetarian. Mili herself always thought the sweet and hot dish could be sweeter. Of course.

The Devil had poured some white wine for Mili and Mardie. He poured himself a generous amount of bourbon into a Collins glass. He didn't usually drink bourbon, but Mili had a bottle of Crown Royal bourbon stashed in case she and Mardie received a surprise visit from

Hugh Everett III. Since there was no whiskey in the house, Lucifer unstashed the bourbon.

"What are our options for Little Mardie?" Mili asked the moment everyone had a drink and a seat at the kitchen table.

Lucifer had heard about Little Mardie's unhappiness up in Heaven from his wife and boys. She missed her family. She missed her friends. She and Arie mourned their dream of sharing a lifetime together farming land from the kibbutz. Satan honestly did not know what could be done. But he would talk to Jehovah again and see what options the Almighty might be open to. It wasn't like it was the only time the Almighty had been faced with a location swap. Mili had, after all, originally gone to Heaven, only to be kicked out and condemned to Hell, so the Old Man was perfectly capable of changing a soul's residency.

He'd ask. He'd bargain. He'd wheedle. He'd do whatever it took to get Little Mardie back home down here. But as sympathetic as he was to his daughter's plight, the far greater issue he was wrestling with right now was how to deal with Osama bin Laden's overwhelming evil. And Muhammad's overwhelming virtue. If his wife had her way, she would have just threatened Bin Laden outright. Very likely the terrorist would have agreed to stop the murderous Saudi forays into Hell if she'd promised him that her husband would immediately put him out of his misery.

"I also can't believe that God left the bullet holes in Little Mardie's back," Mili continued, fuming.

"Not that I support Jehovah's bastardizing moralism," Mardie responded. "But he has a habit of doing that stuff. Remember poor Jesus with the holes in his hands and feet? Have to say I don't really know why God's own son has to endure that."

"They are symbols of suffering," Satan suggested. "Keeps one humble. Remember Osama bin Laden's body? It was so shot up that we would never have known who it was. Or what it was. Just a walking pile of slush. I can't figure out how the hell he can even stand up."

"And on top of all that, he's suffering in the lake of fire," Mardie remarked. "Have to admit though that I am one of those people who thinks that he should be left there forever. In fact, I'd like to stand in front of him and read the names of the men, and the women, and the children who died in the Twin Tower collapses and the planes crashing into them." Mardie shook her head remembering the horror of 9/11. She looked at Lucifer. "And yet Muhammad thinks Bin Laden can be forgiven."

The Devil nodded.

"He thinks *everyone* can be forgiven. It is the central theme of his teachings."

"Geez." Mardie muttered. "What a screwed-up religion."

Mili couldn't help but laugh.

"Yeah, everyone can be forgiven all right," she said. "But only if they have their hair caught on fire for a million years first."

"Sounds exactly like Catholic purgatory," Mardie said.

"Except there's no such place as purgatory," Mili reminded her.

"Yeah. How freakin' weird is all of this?" Mardie responded. "There's no purgatory, but there *is* a real Muslim Jahannam. And while Judeo-Christian Heaven is a place where you can get killed, Judeo-Christian Hell is a place where you can get rich. Or shot to shit by Arabs."

Lucifer smiled and refilled the sisters' glasses with wine and his own glass with bourbon.

"Definitely mindboggling," Mili agreed. "I think that when and if everything gets straightened up around here, I'm going to give a Ted talk."

Mardie laughed so hard she snorted.

Mili grinned.

Lucifer shook his head and smiled.

"So, Let's Talk About What You Believe," Mili told them. "That's what I'm going to call it."

"No one's going to believe anything *you* tell them," Mardie warned and laughed again.

"Back when you and I wouldn't have either!" Mili laughed until tears came to her eyes.

"Ah, the old days," Mardie responded.

"May they never return!" Mili said and lifted her glass. Mardie toasted her and they both reached out and clinked the Devil's glass. Despite everything going on in Hell, Mili and Mardie would never have gone back to London. And Lucifer would never have gone back to Heaven. Thomas Wolfe was right. You can't go home again. Thank goodness.

In the middle of the night Satan's mobile phone vibrated on his night stand. He grabbed it and walked out of the bedroom. The caller ID read Michael Rockefeller. He went downstairs to the living room.

"Yes, Michael," he answered.

"Sorry, sir, to bother you at home at this hour—"

"What hour?" Satan asked.

"Two forty a.m."

"Okay. What's up?"

"A SEAL was attacked in his apartment less than five minutes ago."

"Did he survive?"

"He called in after it was over."

"Always a good sign."

"His name is Chuck Boyk."

"And he served in the Mideast. Part of the Bin Laden raid," the Devil guessed.

"Yes. Two Arabs appeared at his door."

"Didn't knock."

"No, sir. Boyk might have treated them better if they had."

"Right," Lucifer said. "They're both dead?"

"Yes. He took them out with a Russian AEK-971."

Lucifer frowned.

"I though those puppies were rare down here."

"Boyk said to tell you if you asked that he got it from an assassination survivor, Russell Kruckenberg."

Satan nodded. He knew Kruckenberg. Had met him this morning after *he* had survived a Saudi assassination attempt. He had given the dead assassin's AEK to his friend. Greater love hath no SEAL. Lucifer was truly disappointed that Osama bin Laden had sent another team of killers into Hell. But he knew he shouldn't be. Bin Ladin hadn't exactly guaranteed that he'd end the attacks on his killers.

"Michael," he finally said. "Get Job Price over here to my house as soon as possible. Have him gear up and bring his automatic weapon."

"Anything else, sir?" Rockefeller answered.

"Yes. Tell him to bring an extra canteen of water."

CHAPTER NINETEEN

Lucifer greeted Commander Price outside his house. The SEAL was dressed in camouflage khaki fatigues, combat boots, and a helmet. He wore a holstered handgun and an automatic rifle was slung over his shoulder. The Devil was wearing a black T-shirt and black jeans. He wished Bin Laden could see him dressed like one of his Saudi assassins.

"Good evening," Satan said. "Thank you for coming."

Price bowed his head.

"We're going on a mission that you missed."

"Osama bin Laden?"

Lucifer frowned.

"How could you possibly know that?"

"Some demons know angels assigned duty in Muslim Hell," Price answered. "And you know how demons like to gossip."

"So, everyone knows that I went to Jahannam to see Bin Laden today."

Price nodded.

"By all the accounts I heard, the tête-à-tête didn't really produce all the results that you were looking for."

"A gross exaggeration," Satan commented. "My meeting with Bin Laden didn't produce *any* results."

"Word was that the Prophet Muhammad required mercy rather than coercion."

"That part is fair," Lucifer replied. "He believes that Osama has to voluntarily surrender his desire for revenge. Muhammad is probably the saintliest man I have ever met. But when good faces evil, saints don't always triumph."

Price patted his holster. He looked at Satan.

"That's because they don't have guns, sir."

"Right, son," the Devil agreed. "What are you packing?"

Job Price patted his holster again.

"Smith and Wesson Model 29 Classic." He unslung his rifle and held it for Lucifer to see.

"Remington Arms Bushmaster."

Satan nodded.

Price slung the rifle over his shoulder again.

"I think you prepared properly," the Devil told him.

"Do you expect resistance, sir?" Price asked.

"I do not," Lucifer replied. "Bin Laden is the only target, and I will be the one shooting him." Price hadn't noticed any weapons on the Lord of Hell, but it wasn't his habit to interrupt a senior officer.

"At first I considered using a pistol to keep the hit low profile," Lucifer continued. "In fact, I borrowed one from the Archangel Michael before our initial meeting. Then I thought what the hell? So now, I've decided to take him down with a fire bolt. Angel hardware. If something happens to me, *your* assignment is not to leave Jahannam without making sure that Osama bin Laden's Hellion is dead.

"He looks dead. But he only *looks* dead. He is completely disfigured by all the gunshot wounds the SEALs put into his body after they killed him. Your job is to make him as dead as he looks. With Osama gone, the jihadists will lose their icon and their purpose."

Price and Lucifer looked at each other, then nodded. They were partners in a mission to save all the SEALs in Hell, and it made them feel important and powerful. Why did violent solutions to pressing problems always feel so good? Probably because the instinct to employ destructive force had been built into every human being by Jehovah himself. Started with Cain, the first man born in Creation, and the first person to murder another human. He killed his own brother, Abel. And it went from there. Violence had a long history of success. And now it was going to be directed at Osama bin Laden once again.

"Sir?" Price said before they departed. "I received word that you punished a demon and

an Afghan counterspy for plotting my death."

"Yes, I did. A Dominion named Stalker found both traitors and carried out my orders."

"Thank you. You have redeemed my reputation."

"No, I haven't," Lucifer said and smiled. "You're going to do that with me today."

✴ ✴ ✴

Michael came walking toward Lucifer and Job Price as they emerged from the wormhole into the great outer court of Jehovah's temple. He had a curious expression on his face. He shook Satan's hand and introduced himself to Price.

"Michael," he said and extended his hand.

Price gave the Archangel his name and then shook his hand. Michael was impressed by his strength. He was more impressed by the Bushmaster over his shoulder. He looked at Lucifer.

"You're dressed like you're going to play some pick-up basketball," Michael said and grinned. "But let me warn you. The brothers where you are going can kick your ass." The Archangel nodded towards Price. "Your SEAL bodyguard is, however, dressed for success."

"He's not my bodyguard," Satan said. "He's my back-up."

Michael looked from Price to Lucifer and back.

"Who is your target?" he asked.

"Osama bin Laden," Satan said straight out.

"And you're here because you want me to let you access the space opening to Jahannam again."

"Exactly."

"What's in it for me?" Michael asked.

"Got any preferences?" the Devil asked, somewhat charmed by Michael's directness.

"Yes," Michael said. "I want my old job back. All I do here is stand around and watch out for Jehovah. Nothing ever happens. I used to be the one scouring the universe for action. Now look at me. The security detail."

"I would rather be a doorkeeper in the house of God, than dwell in the tents of wickedness," Lucifer said.

"Well, good for you," Michael sneered.

"It's a quotation from the Hebrew scriptures."

Michael shrugged.

"You and Price don't look ready to sweep and mop."

"Oh, but we are," Lucifer told him. "If I return, I will talk to Jehovah about having you trade back roles and responsibilities with Raphael."

After Gabriel's killing, Michael had lost his job as Archangel of destruction and death. Satan could see that he was indeed now wasting away now from boredom.

"You may pass," Michael said considerably cheered up. "You can see the wormhole to Jahannam from here." He pointed. Lucifer could indeed see the slit in space. Michael waved happily. "And come back safe, you hear?"

Lucifer grinned. His hope exactly.

The Devil led Commander Price through the wormhole. One moment they were under Heaven's twilight. The next moment they were in Jahannam's smoky darkness. Lucifer walked toward the lake of fire. Price followed. He didn't speak.

Was he intimidated even a little bit, Satan wondered? Price wasn't going to talk about it if he was. The fact was, though, Job Price was excited. He'd never been anywhere like this before. It was better than any video game he'd played as a kid, or any mission he'd gone on as a SEAL.

At the edge of the lake of fire Lucifer was surprised to see that Osama bin Laden was standing there waiting. For him? He walked up to the pathetic ruin of a once-living human being. Price walked just behind him, having drawn his handgun. Satan stopped in front of Bin Laden.

The terrorist raised his hand to his mechanical voice box and spoke.

"Lord Lucifer," he said.

The Devil nodded and addressed him.

"Two of your soldiers were slain last night during at attack in Hell."

"I know. I am sad to say that I could not stop them. And there will be more to come. My followers show respect, but then they do what they want."

The Devil shook his head. This was not what he had expected.

"I am willing to end the jihad of vengeance," Bin Laden continued. "I will work with Muhammad to relieve my young followers of their hatred and willingness to kill."

"Good luck with that," Lucifer said sincerely. "How can I help?"

"No help is necessary. Simply remain on alert until the attacks cease."

"Which may be never," Commander Price said.

"You may be right," Osama agreed. "But we will try. If Muhammad is right, at the end of time all violence will be banished and we will live in forgiveness."

"Until then," Satan replied, "may you find it in your heart to forgive me for *my* solution to end the violence."

Lucifer raised and pointed his hand at Bin Laden's forehead. Osama stood still and waited. Then he spoke his last words.

"As-salam 'alaykum," he said. Peace be upon you.

The Devil held his arm steady, his hand aimed at Bin Laden's head.

"Wa 'alaykums-salam," he replied. And upon you be peace.

Then Lucifer released a blinding flash of angel power. His lightning bolt completely destroyed Osama bin Laden.

✳ ✳ ✳

Dawn was lightening up the sky when Lucifer walked into his house. All the lights were on and happy laughter was coming from the kitchen. At five thirty in the morning. Usually at this hour his family was sleeping. Except maybe for Sriracha grabbing a smoke. Whose house was he in? He walked into the kitchen.

There was a cake on the kitchen table and a gallon of ice cream. Sriracha, Jesus, and Aunt Mardi were sitting at the table cheering as Mili lifted a big knife to cut the cake. Standing beside her was Little Mardie and Arie. Satan was speechless.

"Darling!" Mili cried and put down the knife.

She turned to go to Lucifer, but Little Mardie cried, "Daddy!" and shot past her. His daughter hugged him so hard it took his breath away. He hugged her back. Mili joined them while everyone clapped. He thought he might be able to survive his unauthorized killing of Osama bin Laden, but kidnapping Little Mardie from Heaven was probably the straw that would break his back.

Everyone sat and Mili sliced up the cake. She was careful to cut around the icing letters that read, "Welcome home, Little Mardie!"

Mili explained what had brought everyone together.

"I woke to hear you leaving the house in the middle of the night," she began. "I was sure that you were going to get Little Mardie, so I dressed and used the wormhole here in the house to follow you to

Heaven. When I stepped out, I went straight to Agatha Christie's house to ask for her help. Little Mardie and Arie were there! I told the kids to follow me and we came straight back here."

Lucifer frowned. He was so dead.

"Didn't you run into Michael up in Heaven?" he asked. "Coming or going?"

"We did. Both ways. When we saw him on the way out, he said he wished Little Mardie and Arie a great visit down here."

Why did Michael allow Mili to enter Heaven, Lucifer wondered? And to willingly let Little Mardie and Arie leave Heaven with Mili? The Archangel was not his friend. Never had been. So why would he let Mili take Little Mardie and Arie? All the Devil could think was that Michael was prepared to do anything necessary to get the Devil to indeed support God giving Michael his old tasks back.

Lucifer would have to explain to Jehovah that Little Mardie had returned to Hell. He'd ask for a Hellion body for her and one for Arie. He'd make sure the bullet holes in Little Mardie's back were gone. What was the point of that lunacy? She was the innocent victim, not the damn shooter. Perhaps God would relent and let the young people stay in Hell after all. Or not. Satan didn't even want to imagine what Jehovah's disapproval would entail.

Lucifer went to Heaven that same day to get things straightened out with God. When he arrived for his appointment, he spoke to Michael.

"Thank you for your help, Michael. The mission was successful."

"I know," Michael told him. "Muhammad is already here talking to Jehovah about your enterprise."

Satan's insides churned. But it didn't matter. He had done what needed to be done knowing that hope for any upside to his action was a long shot.

"What kind of mood is the Old Man in?" he asked Michael.

"Benevolent," the Archangel told him.

Then Jehovah had not yet heard that Mili had taken Little Mardie.

"However things go down today," Lucifer told Michael, "I'm going to advise Jehovah on your desire to have your old job back again. I also think he needs to know that from my vantage point, there are a lot more serious issues occurring in the universe these days because we are lacking your proactive instinct. Finding and slaughtering evildoers."

Michael was taken aback by the Devil's comment.

"Really?" he asked, clearly a little embarrassed.

"Yes," Satan answered. "Between you and Muhammad, Creation might sooner or later clean up into a nice place to live."

Michael nodded. He had no idea how to respond to Lucifer's compliment. He wasn't used to anyone telling him that his widespread killings were something they appreciated.

"By the way," Michael replied. "There are two other folks with Jehovah who want to sit in on your meeting."

Michael didn't tell him who they were and the Devil didn't ask. He didn't have to. He knew who was there. Michael opened the golden doors to the temple and escorted Satan down the long hall to Jehovah's great room.

He announced Lucifer's arrival, then stepped aside. Satan stood in the doorway and gazed inside. God was sitting on his divan. He'd been watching Vatican television. He looked beatific. And why not? He'd been listening to sermons by Pope Francis. And now he was the pontiff's spitting image.

Seated in one of the folding metal chairs sat Muhammad. He smiled at Lucifer. Sitting next to him in a restored, whole Hellion body was Osama bin Laden. He smiled at Lucifer, too.

"Enter, Lucifer Morningstar," Jehovah demanded.

Satan walked in and stood facing God. Jehovah had some things to say to him.

"You embarked on an unauthorized mission into Muslim Jahannam. You countermanded Muhammad's desires to let Osama journey the long path of redemption. You killed his Hellion body and ended his afterlife. What say ye?"

"Guilty," Lucifer pleaded. "My only hope was that in bringing about Osama's second death, his radical followers would have no one left to revenge. I also have to admit that I believed that Muhammad, in imitation of Allah's mercy, would see fit to ask that Osama be restored to a renewed and undamaged Hellion body once he'd heard that he had forsworn his revenge and asked for forgiveness."

"So, your actions were predicated on the time-worn cliché, the end justifies the means?" Jehovah demanded.

Lucifer nodded and hung his head. What a pathetic thing to have to admit. God had his justice. Muhammad had his forgiveness. All he had was the end justifies the means.

Jehovah responded in a normal voice.

"Well," he said jovially, "works for me."

Osama bin Laden smiled again. He wore a robe and a white turban. His face was intact, his hair had been restored, and he had his signature beard with the squared-off bottom. Osama bowed his head deeply to Lucifer. Muhammad nodded approvingly, then looked directly at the Devil and gave him a thumbs up. Lucifer looked again at Bin Laden's beard. It was all coal black. He had read in several SEALs' accounts of the raid that they had found beard dye in Bin Laden's bathroom. Satan grinned. He wouldn't be telling anyone.

Epilogue

Jehovah's guests chatted with each other in his great room. There was an open bar and tapas prepared by one of God's favorite Spanish chefs. The group included all three Archangels, Lucifer, Michael, and Raphael. Both Wickett sisters were there. They were talking with SEALs Don Korpinen and Russell Kruckenberg. Muhammad was there but standing by himself. Most of the guests were listening to Osama bin Laden. Satan smiled. With his voice box, the Saudi had been hardly able to talk. Now with his own voice restored, it seemed like he was never going to stop.

Lucifer walked to a quiet corner to visit with SEAL officer Job Price. The commander was in his dress whites and looked happy.

"Any reflections on your last SEAL mission?" Satan asked Price.

"Well," the commander answered, "I witnessed the Lord of Hell end a war by taking a life in Jahannam. It was a wonder and a privilege to behold."

"It did work out well," the Devil said modestly.

"You'd have made a good SEAL," Price said appreciatively.

Lucifer sipped his whiskey and nodded. That might be the nicest compliment he had ever received.

Jehovah raised his hand. The guests instantly grew quiet.

"Ladies and gentlemen," he said. "Welcome to a night of reconciliation and peace. Our worlds collided and now they have melded. To celebrate this momentous occasion, I have asked a relative newcomer here and a most welcome new saint to sing for us." Jehovah extended his hand toward the open doorway. A svelte black woman walked in. Every guest applauded and cheered.

A towering talent of love and forgiveness, the woman smiled and waved. The crowd went wild. And why not? How often could any party boast the presence of Jehovah and Muhammad, Navy SEALs and Osama bin Laden, Lucifer and both Wickett sisters, Mili and Mardie? And the star belting out her repertoire? Aretha Franklin.

All I'm askin' is for a little respect, Aretha sang,
R-E-S-P-E-C-T, R-E-S-P-E-C-T!

That's what everything is all about, Lucifer thought. Whether it was Earth or Hell, Jahannam or Heaven, all people *really* wanted is a little respect. And maybe some whiskey.

Or wine. Hugs and kisses. A compliment now and again. Pretty simple stuff. He looked across the room and saw Mili watching him. He saw her mouth the words, *I respect you.* He would never think of this song in the same way again.

The End

Acknowledgements

I would like to thank—once again!—the fine professionals who work with me. Mark Meyer of Professional Book Proofreading.

The formatting artists at Wordszworth. And Vincent Chong for his cover design and art.

www.ingramcontent.com/pod-product-compliance
Lightning Source LLC
Chambersburg PA
CBHW070354200726
48294CB00003B/913